DEATH OF A PERFECT WIFE

PERFECT WIFE

A HAMISH MACBETH MURDER MYSTERY

M.C. BEATON

Constable • London

CONSTABLE

First published in the United States in 1988 by St Martin's Press,
175 Fifth Avenue, New York, NY

First published in the UK in 2008 by Robinson,
an imprint of Constable & Robinson Ltd

This edition published in Great Britain in 2017 by Constable

1 3 5 7 9 10 8 6 4 2

Copyright © M. C. Beaton, 1988, 2008

The moral right of the author has been asserted.

A CIP catalogue record for this book
is available from the British Library.

ISBN: 978-1-47212-409-8

Typeset in Palatino by Photoprint
Printed and bound in Great Britain by
CPI Group (UK) Ltd, Croydon, CR0 4YY

Papers used by Constable are from well-managed forests and other
responsible sources.

MIX
Paper from
responsible sources
FSC® C104740
www.fsc.org

Constable
An imprint of
Little, Brown Book Group
Carmelite House
50 Victoria Embankment
London EC4Y 0DZ

An Hachette UK Company
www.hachette.co.uk

www.littlebrown.co.uk

For Rory Stuart

Chapter One

'Will you walk into my parlour?' said a spider to a fly: 'Tis the prettiest little parlour that ever you did spy.'
— Mary Howitt

It was another day like the morning of the world.

Police Constable Hamish Macbeth, his dog at his heels, sauntered along the waterfront of Lochdubh, a most contented man. For two whole weeks the weather had been perfect.

Above was a cerulean sky and before him the bustling little harbour, and beyond that the blue of the sea, incredible blue, flashing with diamonds as the sun sparkled on the choppy surface of the water. Around the village rose the towering mountains of Sutherland, the oldest in the world, benign in the lazy light. Across the sea loch was Gray Forest, a cool dark cathedral of tall straight pines. Early roses tumbled over garden fences and sweet peas fluttered their Edwardian beauty in the faintest of breezes. On the flanks of the mountains, bell heather, the early heather that blossoms in June, coloured the green and brown camouflage of the rising moors with splashes of deepest pink. Hairbells, the bluebells of Scotland, trembled at the roadside among the blazing twisted yellow and purple of vetch and the white trumpets of convolvulus.

As Hamish strolled along, he noticed the Currie sisters, Jessie and Nessie, two of Lochdubh's spinsters, tending their little patch of garden. The garden bore a regimented look. The flowers were in neat rows behind an edging of shells.

'Fine day,' said Hamish, smiling over the hedge. Both sisters straightened up from weeding a flower bed and surveyed the constable with disfavour.

'Nothing to do as usual, I suppose,' said Nessie severely, the sunlight sparkling on her thick glasses.

'And isn't that the best thing?' said Hamish cheerfully. 'No crime, no battered wives, and not even a drunk to lock up.'

'Then the police station should be closed down. The police station should be closed down,' said Jessie, who repeated everything twice over like the brave thrush. 'It's a sin and a shame to see a well-built man lazing about. A sin and a shame.'

'Och, I'll find a murder jist for you,' said

Hamish, 'and then you really will have something to complain about.'

'I hear Miss Halburton-Smythe is back,' said Jessie, peering maliciously at the constable. 'She's brought some of her friends from London to stay.'

'Good time to come here,' said Hamish amiably. 'Lovely weather.'

He smiled and touched his cap and strolled on, but the smile left his face as soon as he was out of sight. Priscilla Halburton-Smythe was the love of his life. He wondered when she had come back and who was with her. He wondered when he would see her. Anxiety began to cast a cloud over his mind. It seemed amazing that the day was still perfect: the sun still shone and a seal rolled about lazily in the calm waters of the bay.

He tried to recover his spirits. The air smelled of salt and tar and pine. He walked on to the Lochdubh Hotel to see if he could scrounge a cup of coffee.

Mr Johnson, the manager, was in his office when Hamish walked in. 'Help yourself,' he said with a jerk of his head towards the coffee machine in the corner. He waited until Hamish was seated over a cup of coffee and said, 'The Willets's place has been sold.'

Hamish raised his eyebrows. 'I wouldnae hae thought anyone would have taken that.' The Willets's house was a Victorian villa set back from the waterfront. It had been up for sale for five years and was in bad repair.

'I gather they got it for a song. Someone said ten thousand pounds was the figure.'

'And who's they?'

'Name of Thomas. English. Don't know anything about them. Expected to move in today. Maybe it'll be work for you.'

Hamish grinned. 'A crime, you mean? With weather like this, nothing bad can happen.'

'The glass is falling.'

'I never knew a barometer yet that could tell the weather,' said Hamish. 'What's happening up at Tommel Castle?' Hamish asked the question with a casual air of indifference, but Mr Johnson was not deceived. Tommel Castle, some miles outside Lochdubh, was the home of Priscilla Halburton-Smythe.

'I gather Priscilla's come back with a party of friends,' said the manager.

Hamish took a sip of coffee. 'What kind of friends?'

'Sloane Rangers, I think. Two fellows and two girls.'

Hamish was conscious of a feeling of relief. It sounded like two couples. He dreaded to hear that Priscilla had brought a boyfriend with her.

'Had a look at them yet?' he asked.

'Oh, aye, they were in for dinner here last night.'

Hamish stiffened. 'And what has happened

to the colonel's hospitality when his daughter has to entertain her friends at the local hotel?'

Mr Johnson looked uncomfortable. 'They've been at the castle for over a week,' he said, and then looked at the ceiling so that he should not see the disappointment in Hamish's eyes.

Hamish put his unfinished coffee slowly down on the desk. 'I'd better be getting off on my rounds,' he said. 'Come along, Towser.' The big mongrel slouched out after his master, his plume of a tail at half-mast as if he sensed Hamish's distress.

Hamish stood out in the forecourt of the hotel among the tubs of scarlet geraniums and blinked in the sunlight. It seemed strange that the weather was still as glorious as ever. Over a week! And she had not called.

He went to the police station and then through the garden at the back and up to his small croft to make sure his sheep had enough water. The sun was hot on his back, curlews piped from the heather and overhead a buzzard, like Icarus, sailed straight for the sun.

A large black ewe ambled up and nuzzled his hand. Hamish automatically patted the sheep, his thoughts on what was going on at the castle. Priscilla had said something teasing last time before she had left about his lazy lack of ambition. He was certainly not an ambitious man. He enjoyed his easygoing life and he loved western Sutherland with its mountains and heather and the broad stretch of the

Atlantic beyond the sea loch where the old people said the blue men rode the waves and the dead came back as seals.

He decided it would do no harm just to go up to the castle and have a look.

He had a new white Land Rover, a perk from head office in Strathbane, no doubt with the blessing of Chief Detective Inspector Blair who enjoyed a reputation for solving murders with Hamish's help, even though Hamish had solved them single-handedly but had let the boorish detective take the credit.

The twisting road up to the castle wound through the hills and his heart lifted as the road bore him higher above the village. There would be some simple explanation as to why Priscilla had not been to see him. Her father, the colonel, strongly disapproved of her friendship with the local bobby. He had probably told her not to have anything to do with him, though Hamish, deliberately forgetting that her father's temper and disapproval had not stopped Priscilla from visiting him in the past.

He parked the Land Rover on the verge outside the gates. He wanted to spy out the lie of the land before he was seen.

He walked slowly up the drive. He could hear shouts and laughter, so instead of following round the turn of the drive that would bring him to the lawns in front of the house, he plunged into the pine wood at the side and

6

made his way silently over the pine needles to where he could get a clear view without being seen himself.

They were playing croquet, Priscilla and her friends. At first, he had eyes only for her. She was bent over the mallet, the golden bell of her hair falling about her face. She was wearing a plain white blouse, a short straight scarlet cotton skirt, and low-heeled brown sandals with thin straps. Hamish's attention turned to the man who had come up to her and put his arms around her to show her how to use the mallet. He was tall, with crisp dark hair, a handsome face, and a blue chin. He was wearing a checked shirt and black curling hairs sprouted at the open neck. His sleeves were rolled up, revealing strong tanned arms covered with black hair.

There were two girls, both with the monkey faces of rich Chelsea, and well-coiffed hair. They were wearing casual clothes. The other man was a rabbity-looking individual with gold-rimmed glasses.

Then as Hamish watched, Priscilla smiled at the dark-haired man, a radiant smile, a happy smile, and Hamish felt cold. A darkness grew inside him. Priscilla Halburton-Smythe was in love with that hairy ape, that Neanderthal. His distress was sharp and acute. Suddenly, the smile left Priscilla's face and she looked about her and then at the trees.

Hamish crept silently away. He felt numb. Misery dragged at his feet like clay as he walked back to the Land Rover.

He drove very carefully back to Lochdubh, drove like a drunk man trying to sober up.

Then he saw a large dusty removal van outside the Willets's house. The newcomers had arrived.

Rather than be alone with himself and his thoughts, Hamish drove straight to the house and parked beside the van. A couple, a tall, rather elegant woman and a big shambling man, were unloading bits and pieces.

'Need any help?' he asked. 'I'm Hamish Macbeth, the local bobby.'

The woman wiped her hand on her trousers and held it out. 'Trixie Thomas,' she said, 'and this is my husband, Paul.'

She was almost as tall as Hamish. She had long brown hair which curled naturally on her shoulders and brown eyes, very large with bluish whites. Her mouth was thin and her teeth, rather prominent when she smiled, very white. Hamish judged her to be about forty-five. Her husband, a large bear of a man with a crumpled clown's face, looked like a fat man who had recently been on a severe diet. His skin looked baggy as if it was meant to stretch across a fatter frame. He had little black eyes and a big mouth and a squashed nose.

'Are you managing?' asked Hamish.

'We're doing our best,' sighed Trixie. 'But it

is hot. We rented this removal van. Couldn't afford the professionals so I suppose we'll have to manage . . . somehow.' Her eyes grew wider and her mouth drooped and her hands fluttered in a helpless gesture.

'I'll give you a hand,' said Hamish. He removed his peaked cap and rolled up the sleeves of his blue regulation shirt.

'Oh, *would* you?' breathed Trixie. 'Poor Paul is so *helpless*.' She had a breathless sort of voice, marred by a faint Cockney whine.

Hamish glanced at Paul to see how he liked being described as helpless but the big man was smiling amiably.

Glad of something to take his mind off his troubles, Hamish worked steadily. He and Paul loaded in the furniture and the bric-a-brac and books while Trixie walked about the house showing them where to put things. 'We'll need more furniture,' she said. 'We're both on the dole and we decided to turn this into a bed and breakfast.'

'Aye, well, if you're quick about it, you might get the tourists for July and August,' said Hamish. 'And if you want any second-hand stuff, there's a good place over at Alness. It's a bit of a drive . . .'

Trixie's mouth drooped again. 'We haven't a penny left for furniture,' she said. 'I was hoping some of the locals might have some bits and pieces they don't want.'

'Maybe I've got something I can let you have,' said Hamish. 'When we've finished, come over to the station and I'll make you something to eat.'

He regretted the invitation as soon as it was out of his mouth. Although by no means a vain man, he had a feeling Trixie was making a pass at him. She was emanating a sort of come-hither sexiness, occasionally bumping into him as if by accident, and giving him a slow smile.

He regretted his invitation even more when the couple arrived at the police station. While he was cooking in the kitchen, Trixie wandered off into the other rooms without asking permission and was soon back, her face a little flushed and her eyes wider than ever. 'I notice you don't use the fire,' she said, 'and there's that old coal scuttle. We don't have a coal scuttle.' She smiled ruefully. 'Couldn't afford one.'

The coal scuttle had been given to Hamish by an aunt. It was an old eighteenth-century one with enamelled panels and he was very fond of it. Her eyes seemed to be swallowing him up and he was surprised at the effort it took to shake his head and say, 'No, I use that the whole time in the winter. You cannae expect me to light fires in a heat wave.'

Trixie was now examining the contents of the kitchen shelves. She lifted down a pot of homemade jam and examined the label.

'Strawberry! Just look, Paul. And homemade. I love homemade jam.'

'Take it with you when you go,' said Hamish. She threw her arms around him. 'Isn't he delightful?' she said.

Hamish extricated himself and served the meal on the kitchen table.

He was beginning to dislike Trixie but he did not yet know why that dislike should be so intense. He turned his attention to Paul. The big man said they had decided to get out of the rat race and come north to the Highlands and maybe earn their living taking in paying guests. 'There's a lot to be done to the house,' he said, 'but it shouldn't take too long to fix, and then I thought I might start a market garden. There's a good bit of garden there.'

'The trouble is,' said Hamish, moving his long legs to one side to avoid Trixie's, which had been pressing against his own, 'that the summers haven't been very good and people have been taking holidays abroad. Mind you, with all the jams at the airports, they were saying on the news that people are starting to holiday in Britain again so you might be lucky.'

'We put advertisements already in the *Glasgow Herald* and *The Scotsman*, advertising accommodation for July and August,' said Trixie.

Hamish thought that for a pair with little money it was odd that they had found enough to advertise. And it was nearly the end of June.

They would need to work very hard to get the rooms ready in time.

When they stood up to go, Trixie said, 'I don't want to be a pest, but if you've any little thing in the way of furniture . . .? I mean, it's all paid for by the government anyway.'

'Only the desk and chair, filing cabinet, and phone in the office are supplied by the police force,' said Hamish. 'The living quarters are all furnished by me. I haven't time to look at the rooms at the moment, but if I find anything, I'll let you know.'

With a feeling of relief, he ushered them out. It was only when he was watching them make their way back to their own house that he realized with something of a shock that the weather had changed. The air felt damp and there was a thin veil of cloud covering the sun. He walked slowly round the front of the police station and stared down the loch.

Rain clouds were heading in from the sea on a damp wind. They were trailing long fingers over the water that had a black oily swell.

And then the midges came down, those Scottish mosquitoes, the plague of the Highlands. All during the long, dry spell, they had been mercifully absent. Now they descended in clouds, getting in his eyes and up his nose. He ran back into the kitchen, cursing, and shut the door.

The idyll was over. The weather had broken, Priscilla had returned with a man, and that couple had moved into Lochdubh, bringing with them an atmosphere of unease and trouble to come.

That evening, Dr Brodie settled down to a large dinner of steak and chips. He and his wife ate at the round kitchen table. He had long ago given up any hope of ever finding it clear. His plate was surrounded by books and magazines and tapes and unanswered letters. The fruit bowl in front of him contained paper clips, hairpins, two screwdrivers, a tube of glue, and a withered orange.

His wife was sitting opposite him, a book propped up against the wine bottle. Dr Brodie surveyed her with affection. She had a thin intelligent face and large grey eyes. Wispy fair hair as fine as a baby's fell across her face and she put up a coal-smeared hand to brush it away. Dr Brodie was a contented man. He enjoyed his small practice in the village and although he sometimes wished his wife, Angela, were a better housekeeper, he had become accustomed to his messy, cluttered home. Angela's two spaniels snored under the table and the cat promenaded on top.

'The cat's just walked across your plate,' commented the doctor.

'Oh, did it? *Shoo!*' said Angela, absent-mindedly, waving a hand and then turning another page of her book.

'There are new people at the Willets's place,' said the doctor, pouring brown sauce over his steak and ketchup over his chips. He pulled away the wine bottle and poured himself a glass. Angela's book fell over.

'I said there are new people at the Willets's place,' repeated her husband.

His wife's dreamy eyes focussed on him. 'I suppose I had better go and welcome them tomorrow,' she said. 'I'll bake them a cake.'

'You'll what? When could you ever bake a cake?'

Angela sighed. 'I'm not a very good house-keeper, am I? But on this occasion, I am going to be good. I bought a packet of cake mix. I can simply follow the instructions.'

'Suit yourself. Priscilla Halburton-Smythe called down at the surgery to pick up a prescription for her father. She drove straight off afterwards.'

'And?'

'Well, she's been back over a week and she hasn't called at the police station once.'

'Poor Hamish. Why does he bother? He's an attractive man.'

'Priscilla's a very beautiful girl.'

'Yes, isn't she,' said Angela in a voice which held no trace of envy. 'Maybe I'll bake a cake for Hamish, too.'

'The fire extinguisher's above the stove, remember,' cautioned her husband. 'The time you tried to make jam, everything went up in flames.'

'It won't happen again,' said Angela. 'I must have been thinking about something else.'

She rose to her feet and opened the fridge door and took out two glass dishes of trifle which she had bought that day at the bakery. The trifle consisted of rubbery custard, thin red jam, and ersatz cream. The doctor ate it with enjoyment and washed it down with Chianti and then lit a cigarette.

He was in his fifties, a slim, dapper little man with a balding head, light blue eyes, a freckled face, and dressed in shabby tweeds that he wore winter and summer.

After dinner, the couple moved through to the living room while the cat roamed over the kitchen table, sniffing at the dirty plates.

The fire had gone out. Angela never raked out the ashes until the fireplace became so full of them that the fire would not light. She knelt down in front of the hearth and began to shovel out piles of grey ash into a bucket.

'Why bother?' said the doctor. 'Light the electric fire.'

'Good idea,' said Angela. She rose to her feet, leaving ash all over the hearth and plugged in the fire and switched it on. Despite the warm weather, their house was always cold. It was an old cottage with thick walls and stone floors. Angela then went back to the table, absent-mindedly patted the cat, picked up her book, returned to the living room, and began to read again.

The doctor had learned to live with his wife's messy housekeeping. He would have been very surprised could he have known that Angela often felt she could not bear it any longer.

Often she thought of getting down to it and giving the place a thoroughly good clean, but a grey depression would settle on her. For relaxation she had once enjoyed reading women's magazines but now she could not even bear to look at one, the glossy pictures of perfect kitchens and fresh net curtains making her feel desperately inadequate.

But on the following morning after she had served up her husband's breakfast – fried black pudding, haggis, bacon, sausages, fried bread and two eggs – she felt a lifting of her heart. She had a Purpose. She would behave as a good wife should and bake a cake and take it over to the new neighbours.

When she settled down to read the instructions on the back of the packet of Joseph's Ready Mix, she experienced a strong feeling of resentment. If it was indeed a 'ready mix' then why did she have to add eggs and milk and salt and all these fiddly things that should have been in the packet already?

She searched around for the cake tin and then remembered the dogs were using it as a drinking bowl. She threw out the water and put the dogs' water in a soup bowl instead, wiped out the cake tin with a paper towel, greased it, and started to work.

That afternoon, she set out for the Willets's place – no, Thomas's place, she reminded herself – feeling very proud of herself. She held in front of her, like a crown on a cushion, a sponge cake filled with cream.

There seemed to be a lot of activity around the old Victorian villa. Archie Maclean, one of the local fishermen, was carrying in a small table, Mrs Wellington, the minister's wife, was cleaning the windows, and Bert Hook, a crofter, was up on the roof, clearing out the gutters.

The front door was open, and Angela walked inside. A tall woman approached her. 'My name's Trixie Thomas,' she said. 'Oh, what a beautiful cake. We adore cake, but what with us being unemployed and living on government handouts, we've had to cut out luxuries like this.'

Angela introduced herself and felt a rush of pride when Trixie said, 'In fact, we're ready for a coffee break. We'll have it now.'

She led the way into the kitchen. Her husband, Paul, was washing down the walls. 'All the poor dear's fit for,' said Trixie in a rueful aside. She raised her voice, 'Darling, here's the doctor's wife with a delicious cake. We'll take a break and have some coffee. Sit down, Angela.'

Angela sat down at a table covered with a bright red-and-white checked gingham cloth. Bluebottles buzzed against the window. 'You should get a spray,' said Angela. 'The flies are dreadful today.'

'I think there's been enough damage to the ozone layer already,' said Trixie. 'What I need are some old-fashioned fly papers.'

She was making coffee in what looked like a brand-new machine. 'I grind my own beans,' she said over her shoulder. Paul was already seated at the table, looking at the cake like a greedy child. 'Now, just a small piece, mind,' cautioned his wife. 'You're on a diet.'

Angela watched Trixie with admiration. Trixie was wearing a sort of white linen smock with large pockets over blue jeans and sneakers. Her sneakers were snow white without even a grass stain on them. Angela tugged miserably at her crumpled blouse, which had ridden up over the waistband of her baggy skirt, and felt messy and grubby.

'Now, for the cake,' said Trixie, bringing out a knife. Paul hunched over the table, waiting eagerly.

The knife sank into the cake. Trixie tried to lift out a slice. It was uncooked in the middle. A yellowy sludge oozed out.

'Oh, dear,' said Angela. 'You can't eat that. I don't know how that could have happened. I followed the instructions on the packet so carefully.'

'It's all right,' said Paul quickly. 'I'll eat it.'

'No, you won't,' said Trixie, giving Angela a conspiratorial 'men!' sort of smile.

'I'm hopeless,' mourned Angela.

'Don't worry. I'll show you how to make one. It's just as easy to make a cake from scratch as it is with one of these packets. And it was a lovely thought.' Trixie moved the cake out of her husband's reach. He gave a sigh and lumbered to his feet and went back to work.

'I can't do anything right,' said Angela. 'I am utterly useless about the house. It's like a rubbish bin.'

'You've probably let it go too far,' said Trixie with quick sympathy. 'Why don't you get someone in to clean?'

'Oh, I couldn't. You see, it's so awful, I'd need to make a start on it myself before any cleaning woman could see what she was doing.'

'I'll help you,' Trixie smiled at Angela. 'I feel we are going to be friends.'

Angela coloured up and turned briefly away to hide the look of embarrassed gratification on her face. She had never fitted in very well with the women of the village. In fact, she had never talked to anyone before about how she felt about her dirty house. 'I really couldn't expect you to help me, Trixie,' said Angela, feeling quite modern and bold because people in the village called each other by their surnames, Mr or Mrs This and That, until they had known each other for years.

'I'll strike a bargain with you,' said Trixie.

'I'll nip back to your house with you and if you can let me have any old sticks of furniture you were thinking of throwing out, I'll take that as payment.'

'Lovely,' said Angela with a comfortable feeling she had not experienced since a child of being taken in hand.

But as they walked to the doctor's house, Angela began to wish she had not let Trixie come. She thought of the ash still spilling over the hearth on to the carpet and of all the sinister grease lurking in the kitchen.

Trixie strode in, rolling up her sleeves. She walked from room to room downstairs and then said briskly, 'Now, the best thing to do is just get started and don't think about anything else.'

And Trixie worked. Her hands flew here and here. She was amazingly competent. Grease disappeared, surfaces began to gleam, books flew back up on the shelves. It was all magic to Angela, who felt she was watching a sort of Mary Poppins at work. She blundered around after her new mentor, cheerfully doing everything she was instructed to do as if the house were Trixie's and not her own.

'Well, we've made a start,' said Trixie at last.

'A start!' Angela was amazed. 'It's never been so clean. I just don't know how to thank you.'

'Perhaps you've got an old piece of furniture you don't want?'

'Of course.' Angela looked about her help-lessly. 'There must be something somewhere.'

'What about that old chair in the corner of your living room?'

'You mean that thing?' The chair was arm-less with a bead-and-needlework cover.

Angela hesitated only a moment. It had been her grandmother's but no one ever sat on it and her gratitude for this new goddess of the household was immense. 'Yes, I'll get John to put it in the station wagon and run it over to you this evening.'

'No need for that.' Trixie lifted it in strong arms. 'I'll carry it.'

Despite Angela's protests that it was too heavy for her, Trixie headed off. Angela fol-lowed her to the garden gate. She wanted to say, 'When will I see you again?' and felt as shy as a lover. Dr Brodie was often away on calls and she spent much of her life alone. She had never worked since the day of her mar-riage to the young medical student, John Brodie, thirty years ago. They had been unable to have children. Angela's parents were dead. She felt she had somehow only managed to muddle through the years of her marriage with books as her only consolation.

Trixie turned at the gate. 'See you tomor-row,' she said.

Angela grinned, her thin face youthful and happy.

'See you tomorrow,' she echoed.

Constable Hamish Macbeth was leaning on his garden gate as Trixie went past, carrying the chair.

'Need any help?' he called.

'No, thanks,' said Trixie, hurrying past.

Hamish looked at her retreating figure. Where had he seen that chair? His mind ranged over the interiors of the houses in Lochdubh. The doctor's! That was it.

He ambled along the road to the doctor's house and went around to the side, no one in the Highlands except the Thomas's bothering to use the front door.

'Come in, Hamish,' called Angela, seeing the lanky figure of the red-haired policeman lurking in the doorway. 'Like a cup of coffee?'

'Yes, please.' Hamish eased himself into the kitchen, and then blinked in surprise. He had never seen the Brodies' kitchen look so clean. Angela bubbled over with enthusiasm as she told him of Trixie's help.

'Was that your chair she was carrying?' asked Hamish.

'Yes, the poor things have very little furniture. They want to start a bed-and-breakfast place. It was just a tatty old thing of my grandmother's.'

Hamish thought quickly. Someone setting up a bed-and-breakfast establishment usually wanted old serviceable stuff. He wondered uneasily whether the chair was valuable. But he did not know anything about antiques.

Flies buzzed about the kitchen.

'I should have kept the door shut,' said Angela. 'Wretched flies.'

'You've got a spray there,' pointed out Hamish.

'These sprays make holes in the ozone layer,' said Angela.

'I suppose so. But it's hard to think of the environment when you haff the kitchen full of the beasties,' said Hamish whose Highland voice became more sibilant when he was upset, and somehow he felt that that remark about the ozone layer originally came from Trixie. And yet Trixie was right, so why should he feel so resentful?

After some gossip, Hamish got up and left. A thin drizzle was falling. The sky was weeping over the loch, but the air was warm and clammy.

And then he saw a Volvo parked at the side of the police station and Priscilla just getting out of it. He broke into a run.

Chapter Two

O Love! has she done this to thee?
What shall, alas! become of me?
                        – John Lyly

He slowed his pace as he neared the police station and tried to appear casual although his mouth was dry and his heart was thumping against his ribs.

Then just before he reached her, his pride came to his rescue. He, Hamish Macbeth, was not going to run after a woman with such abysmal taste that she could become starry-eyed over a man who looked like an ape.

'Evening, Priscilla,' he said.

'Open the kitchen door quickly,' said Priscilla. 'I'm being eaten alive. Why do the midges leave you alone?'

'I'm covered in repellent,' said Hamish. 'The door's unlocked anyway. No need to wait for me. What brings you?'

Priscilla sat down at the kitchen table and pushed back the hood of her anorak. 'Father

25

thought I ought to call on the newcomers,' she said.

Of course, thought Hamish bleakly, and while you're playing lady of the manor, drop in on the local bobby at the same time.

'What did you think of them?' he asked, putting on the kettle.

'They seem very pleasant. She's got quite a forceful personality. Dr Brodie's wife was helping her get things arranged. Mrs Brodie's delighted to find a friend at last, of course.'

'Why of course?' Hamish measured tea leaves into the teapot with a careful hand.

'Mrs Brodie's a lonely woman. She should have been one of those vague academics, writing her thesis and taking yet another degree or doctorate. Lots of brains and no self-confidence and very little commonsense. Trixie Thomas has taken her over with a firm hand. She's going to perm her hair for her tomorrow.'

'She shouldn't have a perm,' said Hamish. 'That baby hair of hers suits her.'

'Oh, well, she's happy and perms grow out,' said Priscilla.

Hamish handed her a cup of tea, poured one for himself, and sat down opposite her at the table.

'And what do you make of the husband, Paul?' he asked.

'Nice man. Bit of a helpless child. Seems

Trixie's got a hard job managing him and all the arrangements for the bed and breakfast.'

'Or that's the way she plays it,' said Hamish. 'Has she asked you for any furniture?'

'As a matter of fact she did. But I told her she'd need to see my father. I don't own any of it.'

'I hear you've been back for over a week.'

Priscilla looked at Hamish's hazel eyes, which were calm and appraising.

'I meant to get down and see you sooner,' she said defensively, 'but time seemed to fly past. I've got these friends up with me. They're leaving tomorrow.'

'Who are they?'

'Oh, just friends. Sarah James and her sister, Janet, David Baxter and John Burlington.'

'I saw them,' said Hamish casually. 'I was driving past. Who's the hairy fellow?'

'You mean the good-looking one with the tanned face? That's John.'

'What does he do?'

'He's a very successful stockbroker.'

'Looks a bit old for a yuppie.'

'Hamish, I wouldn't have thought you would be the type to sneer at yuppies. He's not exactly young, he's thirty.'

'Nearly as old as me,' said Hamish drily.

'Anyway, he's very hard-working and ambitious. He's bought this brill farmhouse in Gloucester for weekends and he's going to take me down to see it when I get back in

27

September. I'm studying computers. My course starts up again in the autumn.'

'And you're in love with him,' said Hamish flatly.

Priscilla coloured up. 'I don't know. I think so.'

All in that moment, Hamish could have struck her. If she had said 'Yes', then that would have been the end of hope and he could learn to be comfortable. But Hamish knew people in love were never in any doubt about it and he cursed her in his heart for the hope she had so unwittingly held out.

He had no claim on her. As far as Priscilla was concerned, they were friends, nothing more.

Priscilla changed the subject. 'After that business in Cnothan, I thought you would have got a promotion.'

'I told you, I don't want a promotion. I've very comfortable here.'

'Hamish, there seems something very ... well ... immature about a man who doesn't want to get on.'

'You're hardly a dynamo of ambition yourself, Miss Halburton-Smythe, or are you just an old-fashioned girl who wants to realize her ambition by marrying an ambitious man?'

'This tea's foul,' said Priscilla. 'And you're foul. You're usually so friendly and pleasant.'

'Priscilla, you haff jist called me an im-

28

mature layabout and you expect me to be pleasant.'

'So I did.' She put a hand on his jersey sleeve. 'I'm sorry, Hamish. Let's start again. I have just arrived, you have just poured me a cup of something made out of sawdust, and we are talking about the Thomases.'

Hamish grinned at her in sudden relief. He prized their usual easygoing friendship and did not want to lose it.

Priscilla smiled back and then sighed. Hamish was tall and gangly and lanky and unambitious. But when he smiled and his hazel eyes crinkled up in his thin face, he seemed part of an older, cleaner world that John Burlington knew nothing about and could never belong to.

'Yes, the Thomases,' she said. 'She's very good at getting one to do things for her. I think half the village has been up at the house already, getting them food and fixing things for them.'

'Where are they from?'

'Edgware, North London.'

'Plenty of jobs in London,' said Hamish. 'Not like the north. Wonder why he's on the dole?'

'Maybe he wasn't. Maybe he threw up his job to come here and went on the dole after he arrived. You're very curious about them.'

'I have an uneasy feeling they are going to cause trouble,' said Hamish slowly.

There was a knock at the kitchen door and Hamish went to open it. John Burlington stood there. 'Is Priscilla here?' he asked. 'I saw her car.'

'I'm here,' called Priscilla, getting to her feet. She introduced the two men. John Burlington's handsome face broke into an engaging smile. 'You've been away for ages, Cilla,' he said. 'The others are outside.'

Priscilla and John left. Hamish wandered through to the office and idly picked up some forms and put them down again. Cilla! What a name. He could hear them laughing outside. He could hear John Burlington saying, 'You'll never guess what our Cilla was doing. Drinking tea with the local copper. Darling, you're too marvellous!' He must have brought the others with him.

Hamish sat down at the desk. He felt he did not really know Priscilla Halburton-Smythe very well. He himself could not have tolerated such company for very long, but then, perhaps jealousy was clouding his judgement.

Dr Brodie sniffed the air suspiciously when he came home that night. Everything seemed to smell of furniture polish and disinfectant. Angela must be worn out with cleaning. Still, he had always wanted a clean house. He sat down at the table.

Angela lifted two boil-in-the-bag curries out

30

of a pan and then the packets of rice. She cut open the bags and tipped the contents on to two plates.

'Where's Raffles?' asked the doctor, ladling mango chutney on to his rice.

'I shut him out in the garden. He will climb on to the table during meals and cats are full of germs.'

'I think over the years we've become immune to Raffles's germs,' said the doctor, pouring a glass of something that was simply emblazoned claret without the name of any vintage to sully its label. 'Why the sudden fear of pollution by Raffles?'

'Trixie Thomas says cats are a menace. Besides, I'm sick of the hairs everywhere.'

'Poor old Raffles,' said the doctor, but his wife had retreated into a book.

He finished his curry. 'Anything for dessert?' he asked. 'The trouble with these instant meals is that they don't fill you up.'

Angela rose from the table. 'I made a butterscotch pudding,' she said. 'Trixie showed me how.'

She put a plate in front of her husband. He took a mouthful and his eyebrows raised in surprise. 'This is delicious,' he said. 'Absolutely delicious. You clever girl.'

'I couldn't have done it without Trixie.'

'Well, God bless Trixie,' said the doctor, looking around the shining kitchen with pleasure.

He was to regret those words bitterly in the weeks to come.

The summer crawled into July. The days seemed long and irritable. Intermittent drizzle and warm wet winds brought the flies and midges in droves. Trixie had made a sign that hung outside the house – The Laurels, Bed & Breakfast. She already had guests, a broken-down looking woman from Glasgow with a brood of noisy, unhealthy children and a thin, quiet man who drifted about the village like a ghost.

Hamish had given the Thomases a wide berth, but one day he saw Paul working in the garden. There was no sign of Trixie so he ambled over.

The big man leaned on his spade when he saw Hamish and said, 'I'm trying to make a vegetable garden. It's hard work. This ground hasn't been turned over for years.'

'Where's Mrs Thomas?' asked Hamish.

'Oh, off somewhere. Inverness, I think.'

'That's verra hard work,' said Hamish sympathetically. 'Archie Maclean's got a rotary cultivator, you know, one of those things that just churn up the earth. If he's not out fishing, I suppose he would lend it to you. Would you like to walk along to his house and we'll ask him?'

'That would be great.' Paul threw down the

spade and wiped his hands on his trousers and came out of the garden to join Hamish.

'You must find Lochdubh a bit of a change from London,' said Hamish, taking out a stick of midge repellent and wiping his face with it.

'I think I can make something of it here,' said Paul. 'New start. Never been able to do much with my life. Trixie's a marvel. I don't know what I would do without her.'

'What was your job in London?'

'Oh, this and that. Trouble was, I'd got so fat, I couldn't move, and the fatter I got, the more I felt I had to eat. Trixie came into my life like a whirlwind and took me over and put me on a diet. I owned the house I lived in. It had been my mother's. Trixie suggested we put it up for sale and buy something up here with the money. I hope I can make something of the garden. It would mean a lot to me to be able to grow things, know what I mean?'

Hamish nodded, and then said, 'But don't you miss the theatres and cinemas and all the fun of the city?'

'No, I didn't have much fun. It's quiet here and the people are friendly. We've had such a lot of help. But that's Trixie for you. Everyone loves her. She's going to do a lot for the village. She's forming the Lochdubh Bird Watching and Bird Protection Society. The first meeting's at the church tonight.'

'It'll be an interest for the children,' said Hamish cautiously. 'It doesn't do to go too far with this bird thing. Some of these societies can be downright threatening, telling people they can't dig the peats because that's the nesting place of the greater crested twit, or something. But I suppose Mrs Thomas is just interested in finding out about the different types of birds.'

'I suppose,' echoed Paul. 'But she likes to do things thoroughly. She's even starting a Clean Up Lochdubh campaign.'

'Morals?'

'No, litter.'

Hamish looked along the street which bordered the waterfront. There was not a scrap of paper in sight.

'And she's going to see Dr Brodie about starting an Anti-Smoking League.'

'My, my, she'll be on dangerous ground there,' said Hamish. 'The doctor smokes like a chimney.'

'I know. Trixie says it's a disgrace. She says he's giving all his patients cancer. And she's had to talk to Angela about the doctor's diet. You should see what she's been feeding that man. Chips with everything. Too much cholesterol.'

Hamish felt uncomfortable. 'It doesn't do to interfere with people,' he said. 'Brodie's fifty-seven and looks about forty and he's never had a day's illness that I can remember.'

'Oh, Trixie knows what's best for him,' said Paul easily.

They walked on in silence. Hamish remembered David Currie, a thin, weedy man who used to live in Lochdubh. He had a tyrant of a mother whom he adored. 'Mother knows best', was his favourite expression. Then one night he had got drunk and had chased his mother down the street with an axe and Hamish had had to rescue the terrified woman. After that, the Curries had moved to Edinburgh. Hamish had heard that David was a leading light in the Jehovah's Witnesses.

Archie Maclean was at home. He gave Hamish a welcoming smile and then the smile faded as he saw Paul behind Hamish. He agreed to lend them his cultivator but he was decidedly chilly towards Paul and Hamish wondered why.

Hamish and Paul worked amiably together throughout the afternoon. Hamish then asked him back to the police station for tea. He put the teapot, two mugs, and a plate of chocolate biscuits on the kitchen table and then the phone in the office rang.

He left Paul and went to answer it. It was Detective Chief Inspector Blair from Strathbane. 'How's the local yokel?' asked Blair.

'Chust fine,' said Hamish.

'Anything going on there?'

'No, nothing.'

'You lucky sod,' grumbled Blair. 'Look, the new super, Peter Daviot, is coming over to the

Lochdubh Hotel for the fishing. I want you to keep oot o' his way.'

'Why?'

'For yir own good, you pillock. If he finds you're daein' nothing, he'll close down your polis station.'

'Anything else?' asked Hamish.

'No,' growled Blair. 'Keep away from Daviot. Ah'm warning ye.'

He slammed down the phone.

Hamish waited a moment and then phoned Mr Johnson, the manager of the Lochdubh Hotel.

'How would you like a supply of free-range eggs for a month for nothing?' asked Hamish.

'I'd like it fine,' said the manager. 'With this salmonella scare, everyone keeps asking for free-range eggs. Of course, I've been telling them they're free range. I get cook to dip them in coffee to turn them brown and stick a wee hen's feather on some of the shells to make it look like the real thing but it would be just my luck if one of them got the food poisoning. What d'you want in return?'

'Is a Mr Daviot in the hotel?'

'Yes, just arrived.'

'Then I want dinner for two this evening,' said Hamish.

'All right. You're on. But don't order champagne.'

Hamish then phoned Tommel Castle. The butler answered the phone and Hamish asked to speak to Priscilla. 'Who is calling?' asked the butler suspiciously. 'James Fotherington,' said Hamish in impeccable upper-class accents.

'Certainly, sir,' oiled the butler.

Priscilla came to the phone. 'Hello, Hamish,' she said. 'It is you, isn't it?'

'Yes, will you have dinner at the Lochdubh with me tonight?'

There was a long silence and Hamish gripped the phone hard.

'Yes,' said Priscilla at last. 'But we'll go Dutch. Johnson's prices get higher and higher.'

'I haff the money,' said Hamish in offended tones.

'Very well. What time?'

'Eight. And ... er ... Priscilla, could you wear something grand?'

'Any point in asking why?'

'No.'

'All right. See you.'

Hamish went back into the kitchen. Paul had gone. So had all the biscuits. Not only that, but there were smears of jam on the plate. Eating chocolate biscuits with jam, marvelled Hamish. It's a wonder that man has any teeth left.

That evening, Dr Brodie sat down to a plate of pink wild rice. His wife poured him a glass of Perrier. 'What's this?' he asked, pushing the mess with his fork. 'Tuna fish rice,' said

Angela proudly. 'You put a can of tuna in the blender and just mix the paste with the wild rice. Try the whole wheat bread. I baked it myself.'

Dr Brodie carefully put down his fork. He looked at his wife. Her hair was all curly, like a wig, and highlighted with silver streaks. She was wearing a white smock with strawberries embroidered on it, a pair of new blue jeans, and very white sneakers. He had not complained once about all the changes, pleased that his wife had all these new interests but hoping she would tire of it all and revert to her normal self. But it had been a long and tiresome day. He was hungry and he was weary. His home sparkled like a new pin but felt sterile and uncomfortable.

He put down his fork and got to his feet.

'Where are you going?' asked Angela.

'I am going to the Lochdubh Hotel for a decent meal. I hear they've got a new chef. Like to come?'

'Don't be ridiculous,' said Angela, tears starting to her eyes. 'I've been slaving all day, getting the place clean, making the bread . . .'

Dr Brodie went out and very quietly closed the door behind him.

Angela sat down and cried and cried. Trixie had said he was killing himself with all that junk food and cheap wine and cigarettes. She had done it all for him and he had sneered at her. At last, she dried her eyes. There was the

Bird Society meeting. Trixie would be there and Trixie would know what to do.

Mrs Daviot said to her husband, 'That's a distinguished-looking couple.'

The superintendent looked over the top of his menu. A tall thin man with flaming red hair in a well-cut but slightly old-fashioned dinner jacket was ushering in a tall blonde who was wearing a strapless jade green gown with a very short ruffled skirt and high-heeled green silk shoes. The waiter came up to take the Daviots' order. 'Visitors, are they?' asked Mr Daviot, indicating the couple.

'Oh, no,' said the waiter, 'that's Miss Halburton-Smythe and Mr Macbeth, the local constable.'

'Ask them to join us,' said his wife eagerly. Mrs Daviot was a social climbing snob and longed to be able to tell her friends that she had had dinner with one of the Halburton-Smythes.

Soon Hamish and Priscilla were seated at the superintendent's table. 'I think it would be better if we just stuck to first names,' said Mrs Daviot eagerly. 'I'm Mary and my husband is Peter.'

'Very well then,' said Priscilla. 'It's Priscilla and Hamish.'

Hamish cursed the impulse that had led him to waste a whole evening, when he could have

39

been alone with Priscilla, in spiting Blair. Mary Daviot was a small, fat, fussily dressed woman whose Scottish accent was distorted by a perpetual effort to sound English. Her husband was small and thin with grey hair, grey eyes, and a grey face. 'So you're Macbeth,' he said surveying Hamish.

'Do call me Hamish, Peter,' said Hamish sweetly.

There was a silence while they all decided what to have to eat. 'The prices are ridiculous here,' said Mr Daviot finally. He turned to the waiter, 'We'll all have the set menu.'

'Perhaps you would care for something else,' said Hamish to Priscilla.

'No, darling,' said Priscilla meekly.

Hamish knew she was angry with him for having used her in order to introduce himself to the superintendent and his heart sank.

'All ready for the Glorious?' Mrs Daviot asked Priscilla.

Priscilla raised her eyebrows.

'I mean The Glorious Twelfth,' explained Mrs Daviot.

'I suppose my father is,' said Priscilla. 'I don't shoot anymore. Few enough birds as it is.'

Hamish ordered a good bottle of claret. 'We'll just have a glass of yours,' said Mr Daviot when Hamish offered him the wine list.

'You were involved in that murder case where that chap was shot on the grouse moor, weren't you?' the superintendent asked Hamish.

'Yes.'

'Tell me about it. I wasn't in Strathbane then.'

As Hamish talked, Priscilla endured the coy and vulgar conversation of Mrs Daviot.

The first course arrived. It was salmon mousse. A tiny portion moulded into the shape of a fish with a green caper for an eye stared up at Hamish.

'I gether the chef is famous for his novel kweezin,' said Mrs Daviot.

'I'm not a fan of nouvelle cuisine,' said Priscilla. 'They never give you enough to eat.'

She glanced at Hamish who seemed to be enjoying himself talking to the superintendent. Hamish did not like Mr Daviot much but found him an intelligent policeman.

Priscilla realized with a shock that she had not thought about John Burlington in recent days. But now she wished with all her heart that he would miraculously turn up and take her out of the dining room and away from Mrs Daviot's greedy eyes that seemed to be pricing her gown, her earrings, and her necklace.

The next course was Tournedos Bonnie Prince Charlie. A small piece of fillet steak rested on a small round of toast. Two mushrooms and two radishes cut in the shape of flowers decorated the plate. A kidney-shaped side dish contained a small portion of sliced carrots and an even smaller portion of mange

41

tout. Hamish mentally cut down the supply of free-range eggs by two-thirds and cast a hurt look at Mr Johnson who came hurrying up.

'Everything all right?' he asked. There was a crash behind him and he swung round. Dr Brodie had upset his chair and was storming from the dining room.

'Excuse me,' muttered Mr Johnson and went after the doctor.

'So it looks as if they'll be no more murders in Lochdubh?' said Mr Daviot.

'I hope so,' said Hamish. 'But we have a creator of violence in our midst.'

'What's thet?' asked Mrs Daviot.

'It's someone who sets up situations and animosities in people that often lead to murder.'

'I don't believe in that sort of thing,' said Mr Daviot. 'Murderers are usually on booze or drugs or both. Or there's the ones that are born bad. No one makes another person murder them.'

'I think they do,' said Priscilla. 'It's often a way of committing suicide. You don't do it yourself but you drive someone else into doing it for you.'

'I never let popular psychology interfere with police work,' said the superintendent. 'Nothing beats a good forensic lab and this genetic fingerprinting is a wonder.'

He and Hamish fell to discussing cases which had been solved by genetic fingerprinting and Priscilla was again left to talk to Mrs Daviot. This is what life would be like were I married to Hamish, she thought. But surely the fact that Hamish had sought out the superintendent meant that he was showing signs of ambition at last. Suddenly cheered, Priscilla endured Mrs Daviot's questioning.

The last course arrived. Flora Macdonald's Frumenty. It tasted to Priscilla like whipped cream with a dash of cooking sherry.

'We must meet up again soon,' Priscilla realized Mrs Daviot was saying.

Priscilla hesitated. She did not want to have to endure the company of this woman again. On the other hand, if Hamish had taken a step towards promotion, then she should help him. Besides, her father would be delighted to meet the new superintendent.

'Come for dinner tomorrow night,' she said. 'Eight o'clock. Tommel Castle. Do you know the way?'

'Oh, yes,' breathed Mrs Daviot. 'Peter, Priscilla's asked us for dinner tomorrow night.'

'That's very kind of you,' said Mr Daviot.

'Yes, thank you, Priscilla,' said Hamish, quickly including himself in the invitation.

Priscilla wondered what her father would say about having Hamish Macbeth as a dinner guest.

When the dinner was over, Mr Daviot signed his bill and Hamish told the waiter airily he would settle his with Mr Johnson in the morning.

On the way out, Hamish fell back a little behind the others. 'What did you think of your meal?' asked Mr Johnson.

'You auld scunner,' said Hamish furiously. 'I'm starving. That was child's portions. It's worth half a dozen eggs and that's all you're going to get.'

'Keep your hair on, laddie. The nouvelle cuisine is now being replaced by vieille. Brodie nearly had a heart attack with rage. Says the whole of Lochdubh's out to starve him.'

'Aye, well, the fish and chip shop will be doing a grand trade tonight.'

Hamish caught up with the others, said goodbye to the Daviots and then escorted Priscilla to her car.

'That was a disgusting meal, Hamish,' said Priscilla. 'But I forgive you all. I never thought to see the day when you would attempt to court a superintendent. High time you decided to do something with your life.'

Hamish hesitated. He dare not tell her he had only done it to spite Blair. She kissed him lightly on the cheek and climbed into her car. 'Want a lift?'

'No, I'll walk.' Hamish raised a hand in farewell and she drove off.

As he strolled along the waterfront, he suddenly saw a figure hurrying along the pavement on the other side of the road. The figure had an anorak hood pulled well over the head, but by those gleaming sneakers, he was sure it was Trixie. She turned her head away as if hoping not to be recognized. He turned and watched her. She was heading for the hotel.

He wondered what she was up to. She appeared to have taken over the gardening from Paul, who could often be seen sitting on the wall outside his house, staring at the loch. Then he forgot about her and wondered instead how Colonel Halburton-Smythe was taking the news that Hamish Macbeth had been invited to dinner.

'Ask the super and his wife by all means,' the colonel was raging, 'but I will not have that scrounging bobby in this house.'

'In that case,' said Priscilla coolly, 'I shall just have to take them all out to a restaurant. Daviot will be very disappointed not to find Hamish at the dinner.'

Jenkins, the butler, who had been serving the colonel's supper of whisky and sandwiches, bent and whispered something in the colonel's ear. The colonel looked startled and left the room followed by his butler. He returned a few moments later, looking very pleased about something, and said, 'Maybe I was too harsh, Priscilla. Ask your local bobby by all means.'

What had Jenkins said, wondered Priscilla. The butler loathed Hamish. Her father's change of heart meant that Jenkins had told him something that had led the colonel to believe that Hamish would be unable to attend that dinner. It was no use asking Jenkins what he had said. Jenkins did not like her either.

She waited until Jenkins came back in with the coffee and slipped out and went down to the cook-housekeeper's parlour, halfway down the backstairs.

Mrs Angus, the cook-housekeeper, was slightly drunk, but then, that was her usual condition. Priscilla told her about the dinner and discussed the menu and then said, 'Does Jenkins know something about Hamish Macbeth? I've got a feeling he doesn't expect him to attend.'

'That's right,' said Mrs Angus in her hoarse whisky voice. 'Jamie, the water bailiff, told someone that Hamish Macbeth was going out poaching on the river tonight. You ken how Hamish and Jamie have the understanding, for Hamish aye takes just the one fish. Bigmouth Jamie was joking tae someone about the local copper being a poacher and that someone has reported it to that Mr Daviot.'

'Who would do a thing like that? No one in the village, surely. Jenkins?'

'Cannae be him. He's been here all evening. But Hamish is to be on that river at midnight and probably that's when this superintendent will go looking for him.'

Priscilla looked at the clock. Eleven-thirty! She ran to her room and changed into a sweater and tweed skirt and flat shoes and then climbed out of the back window so her father should not see her leave, got in her car, and roared off in search of Hamish.

The police station was in darkness and there was no reply to her knock so she drove off again in the direction of the River Anstey.

She parked the car and headed up the track beside the river to Hamish's favourite beat. A thin drizzle was beginning to fall.

Hamish waded into the river and started to cast. The water gurgled about his waders and the wet air smelled of pine, bell heather, and honeysuckle. And then he heard someone crashing down through the undergrowth from the path. He reeled in his line and was making for the opposite bank when a familiar voice stopped him in his tracks. 'Hamish!'

'Priscilla?'

Hamish waded towards the voice. He could see the white blur of her face.

'Get out of there,' hissed Priscilla. 'Someone's told the super about your poaching and he's probably coming to arrest you. Get out! Give me your rod and net and I'll hide them in the bushes. Get your waders off.'

Hamish handed her the rod and net and then sat down on the bank and pulled off his waders. Priscilla emerged from the undergrowth and took the waders and went off to hide them with rod and net.

'Hadn't we better just go?' said Hamish when she came back.

'Listen!'

Priscilla stood close to him and they listened in silence. Then they heard furtive little sounds, the scrape of a foot, the crackling of a twig.

'We'd better look like a courting couple,' said Priscilla. 'Put your arms around me.'

Hamish gathered her close. His senses were reeling. 'Better make a good show of it,' he muttered and bent his head and kissed her.

The world went spinning off. He was whirling off into infinity with Priscilla in his arms. And then a blinding light was shone on his face. He and Priscilla broke free.

Hamish stood dazed, rocking slightly on his heels.

'What is the meaning of this?' he heard Priscilla demanding in arctic tones, but that voice seemed to be coming from a very long way off.

'I'm awfully sorry,' he heard Mr Daviot reply. 'Really very sorry. Jamie said there was a poacher on the river, and . . .'

'As you can see, Mr Daviot, it is all very embarrassing. Jamie, I'm surprised at you,' said Priscilla. The water bailiff shuffled his feet.

'Well, I'm sorry to have interrupted your . . . interrupted . . . er . . .' said the superintendent.

'Exactly. Good night, Mr Daviot. I shall expect to see you and Mrs Daviot at dinner at eight.'

'Yes, well, erm, good night, er, Hamish.'

But Hamish was standing with a vague smile on his face looking at nothing.

After they had gone, Priscilla bustled about, getting the fishing tackle and the waders, avoiding looking at Hamish. The intensity of that kiss and her own reactions had alarmed her. It was all very well to help Hamish on the road up the police ladder, but she had no intention of marrying him. She did not belong to his world or he to hers. At last, she tugged at his sleeve as though to wake him from a dream and he meekly took the things from her and followed her back up the hill.

Chapter Three

*The pursuit of perfection, then, is the
pursuit of sweetness and light . . .*
                    – Matthew Arnold

Detective Chief Inspector Blair had said
Hamish was half-witted. At the dinner at
Tommel Castle that night, Mr Daviot began to
think Blair was right. Hamish tripped over
things, knocked over things, absentmindedly
put his elbow in the gravy boat, and had a silly
sort of smile on his face the whole time.

Mr Daviot sympathized with the colonel,
who appeared to dislike the local policeman
intensely. What on earth did Priscilla see in
the man?

Priscilla Halburton-Smythe was wearing a
short black slip of a dinner gown. It showed
off her slim figure and set off the pale gold of
her hair. Mr Daviot wished his wife had not
chosen to wear beige silk with an enormous
bow on one plump hip. He was used to his
wife's genteel tones, but during that dinner

party, they grated on his ear. Why could she not say *glass* instead of *gless*, or *that* instead of *thet*? He became very cross with her and to most things she said, he interrupted with, 'Don't be silly', or, 'No one's interested in that', until his hurt wife became as clumsy and gauche as Hamish.

In all, it was an unpleasant dinner party for all but Hamish, who seemed off in another world. Mrs Halburton-Smythe, always nervous of her husband's rages, sat like a silent ghost at the head of the table.

Conversation turned to the Thomases. 'Pretty thing, Mrs Thomas,' said the colonel. 'Called here today looking for bits of furniture. Brave woman. Struggles on down there with that oaf of a husband leaving her to hold the place together.'

'Did you give her anything?' asked Priscilla.

'I gave her that old pine washstand. It was stuck in the corner of the tack room covered in dust.'

'She seems very selective,' commented Priscilla. 'That washstand's Victorian. If she's so hard up for furniture, you would think she would be after chests of drawers or beds or something.'

'Oh, she is. You know old Mrs Haggerty who died last year and no one turned up to collect her bits and pieces out of that cottage? Turns out she hasn't any relatives and the cottage belongs to the estate anyway. I promised to drive Mrs Thomas over to have a look at what's there.'

'I would keep clear of her if I were you,' said Priscilla. 'I don't like her much. I think she's a bossy bitch.'

'Mind your language, girl, and when did you start to become such a good judge of character?' The colonel flashed a vicious look at Hamish Macbeth.

Everyone except Hamish was glad when the evening was over. He was still floating above the ground on the memory of that kiss.

But reality crept back into Hamish's mind the following morning. He had kissed Priscilla. She had not kissed him. She had only allowed him to kiss her because the water bailiff and the superintendent were shortly to arrive on the scene. He thought of the dinner party and felt it was like looking back on a party where one had been very drunk.

Flies were buzzing around the kitchen and he seized the fly spray, mentally damning Trixie and her ozone layer, and slaughtered the lot. But the fly spray smelled so vile that he opened the kitchen door to let the air in and five bluebottles promptly flew in, followed by a posse of midges.

The doorbell went at the front of the police station. When he opened the door, a middle-aged couple were standing on the step. 'We're touring Scotland,' said the man in an American accent. 'I'm Carl Steinberger and this is my wife. The hotel here is too pricey for us. We wanted to know if you knew of anywhere cheaper.'

Hamish did not want to put any custom Trixie's way, but, on the other hand, she had the reputation of being a good housekeeper and a good cook. 'There's The Laurels,' he said, pointing along the road. 'It's a bed and breakfast, but if you want lunch, I'm sure Mrs Thomas will arrange something. Come ben and have a cup of tea.' Hamish adored American tourists, feeling more of an affinity with them than the English ones.

He slammed the kitchen door, muttering about the flies. 'You're unlucky,' he said to the Steinbergers. 'It was lovely in June. This weather's miserable. Hot, wet and clammy and the flies are a menace.'

'I don't know why you don't have screen doors like they do in the States,' said Mr Steinberger.

'Screen doors?' Hamish stood with the teapot in one hand.

'Yes. All you need is a wood frame and some metal gauze or you could even use cheese cloth. Anything. Or strings of beads like they have in the Mediterranean countries.'

'Well, I neffer,' said Hamish. 'Such a simple idea. I'll get to work on it today.'

Mr Steinberger looked amused. 'Doesn't look like you've got much crime in this area to keep you occupied.'

'We have had the murders,' said Hamish grandly. He served the couple tea and scones and they chatted amiably. When they left, Mr Steinberger insisted on taking a photo of Hamish at the door of his police station. Rambling roses rioted over the porch, nearly obscuring the blue lamp. 'They'll never believe this back home,' he said.

Hamish went out to a shed in the garden and ferreted out some pieces of wood. Then he went to the drapers and bought cheese cloth. It was the sort of drapers that still sold cheese cloth.

He measured the doorway and then got to work. The rain had stopped and the sun blazed down and the flies buzzed about the kitchen.

Trixie Thomas appeared on the doorstep. 'What do you want?' asked Hamish sharply, for he was sure it was Trixie who had reported his poaching activities to the superintendent.

'I wanted to know if I could go up to your field and collect sheep wool from the fences.'

'Whatever for?'

'Mrs Wellington has given me an old spinning wheel and I'm going to spin yarn.'

'Do you know how to do it?' asked Hamish curiously.

'Oh, yes, I once had lessons from a New Zealand woman at the Women's Cultural Awareness Group in Camden Town in London.'

Hamish groaned inwardly. He knew Trixie would go 'on stage' with her spinning wheel as soon as possible, probably taking it out to the front garden where all could see and marvel at this further example of domestic perfection. She made no move to leave and he asked sharply, 'Anything else?'

'I wanted to know if you would like to come to our Anti-Smoking League meeting tonight?'

'If there is one thing that will keep a man smoking,' said Hamish bitterly, 'it's folk like you going on at him. Why don't you leave Dr Brodie alone?'

'Because he is a doctor and should know better.'

'You must have been a smoker yourself once,' said Hamish. 'There is nothing mair vicious than an ex-smoker.'

Hamish himself was an ex-smoker and had vowed never to give in to the strong temptation to reform people who were still smoking. Trixie opened her mouth to say something and then thought better of it. She was feeling in a good mood. Colonel Halburton-Smythe had driven her over to an old deserted cottage and she had made quite a good haul. The colonel had entertained her with his worries about the possibility of his daughter perhaps marrying Hamish Macbeth.

'Mind if I use your toilet?' asked Trixie.

'Oh, very well,' said Hamish, standing aside to let her past.

She was gone a long time and he was just about to go in search of her in case she was searching the rooms when he heard her voice from the front of the house, 'I see Paul. I'll let myself out this way.'

Hamish went back to work. She seemed to have forgotten about collecting wool from the fences. His dislike of Trixie, he realized, was mainly because of the change she had wrought in Angela Brodie. Angela with her ridiculously curly hair now wore a perpetually harried look and was thinner than ever.

He finished the door and then discovered he needed hinges and set off in the direction of the ships chandlers which was also the local ironmongers and which was down by the harbour. As he was passing The Laurels, he heard a faint humming sound and looked into the garden. Sure enough, Trixie was there, busily spinning, a self-important look on her face. He went on his way and met one of the local fishermen, Jimmy Fraser. 'What about a pint, Hamish?' asked Jimmy. 'I'm buying.'

'All right,' said Hamish. They walked into the pub at the side of the Lochdubh Hotel. 'What's the matter, Jimmy?' asked Hamish. 'I can practically see the steam coming out your ears.'

'It's that wumman,' growled Jimmy.

'Which one?'

'Her. The Englishwoman. Archie Maclean took herself out in the boat last night. A wumman on a boat! It iss a wunner we didnae drown. Forbye, when I lit a cigarette, she struck it oot o' my mouth, and when I went to belt her one, Archie said I wass to leave her alone and he iss the skipper. It's a black day. They'll be trouble from this.'

'And why was Archie Maclean taking herself out on his boat?'

'Soft about her, that's what he iss. Sitting there, holding her hand like a great bairn and leaving uss to do all the work.'

'And what has Mrs Maclean to say to this romance?'

Jimmy looked alarmed. 'We wouldnae tell her. She'd kill that wumman if she knew.'

After a while, Hamish left him, bought the hinges, and walked back to the police station. So the perfect wife had fallen off her pedestal. Mrs Maclean was not popular but the Lochdubh women would not like an Englishwoman poaching one of their own, so to speak.

Therefore, it was with some surprise that he saw later that day the minister's wife, Mrs Wellington, carrying a cake to the Thomases. He was out walking with Towser when he saw her leaving. 'Afternoon, constable,' she called. Hamish strolled up to her. 'Been visiting the scarlet woman?' he said.

'Whatever do you mean, Mr Macbeth?'

Hamish was a gossip, but hardly ever a malicious one. He decided to make an exception in this case. 'Why, it is all over the village how herself went out with Archie Maclean and held his hand.'

Mrs Wellington was a large tweedy woman. She eyed Hamish with disfavour. 'And it is all over the village how you were caught up on the Anstey in the middle of the night, kissing and canoodling with Miss Halburton-Smythe.'

'Yes, but I am not the married man.'

'Meaning Archie Maclean is? Shame on you, Mr Macbeth. Trixie and Paul told me all about it. Paul was laughing like mad. He said Trixie had gone out just to get some free fish – for the lambs are so desperately poor – and Archie got all spoony and she didn't know how to handle it. Paul said there's always some fellow or another who's spoony about her. So if you hoped to turn me against her, you've failed. She's the best thing that ever happened to Lochdubh, which is more than I can say about a certain lazy gossiping constable.' And quite red in the face with indignation, Mrs Wellington strode off.

'Now what do you make of that?' said Hamish to Towser. Towser snorted. 'Exactly,' said Hamish. 'Fair makes you sick.'

The Thomases had another battered-looking woman in residence with her brood of noisy children. Hamish wondered whether they got welfare cases to fill the rooms. An unmarried mother with four children would rake in quite a large government benefit. The thin quiet man seemed to be a perpetual lodger. Hamish saw him coming and said, 'Good afternoon', but the man muttered something and shied away.

The next morning, Dr Brodie poked around a bowl of something and said to his wife, 'I know you're interested in the protection of birds but there is no need to serve me their droppings for breakfast.'

'That's muesli,' said Angela in aggrieved tones. 'It's good for you.'

Dr Brodie looked at her. 'I suppose Trixie told you to serve it to me.'

'She showed me how to make it up from oatmeal and raisins and nuts,' said Angela eagerly. 'It's so much cheaper than the packet kind and better for you.'

'That woman turned up in my waiting room yesterday and put non-smoking stickers all over the walls without asking my permission. I wasn't going to tell you about it and worry you but enough is enough. I told her to get knotted and so she is writing to the health authorities to complain about me.'

Angela's loyalty was shaken.

'Doctors shouldn't really smoke, dear. You can't really blame her . . .'

Her voice trailed off before the fury in her husband's eyes. 'Listen to me,' he said. 'I've put up with your Trixie nonsense because I thought it was a passing fad. But my home has become a sterile hospital ward, the cat's shut in the shed and the dog's in a kennel in the garden. My wife has a hairstyle like Chico Marx and dresses like one of those tiresome women who are always going on marches and demonstrating something. I want steak and chips for dinner and a bottle of wine. Put any more rabbit food in front of me and I will puke all over the table. And I want to see the animals in the house this evening. Mention that woman's name to me again and I will kill her.'

Mrs Maclean hit her husband on the head with a jug when he entered the house. He reeled back, screaming, 'What was that fur?'

Although the residents of Lochdubh had not directly told her about her husband and Trixie, they had told her in that sideways Highland way of communicating nasty information, apocryphal stories about men they had known who had become silly over English women, and Mrs Maclean, being equally Highland, had been able to transcribe the coded messages.

'You've been making up tae that English woman, ye daft wee scunner,' yelled Mrs Maclean.

'She jist wanted a trip out in ma boat,' he said sulkily, rubbing his head.

'And you held her hand, like a daft school-boy! Listen tae me, Archie Maclean, you go near that wumman again and I'll strangle her wi' ma bare hands.'

'You're haverin',' said Archie, running out of the door before she could hit him again.

He made straight for the pub where Jimmy Fraser was already propping up the bar. Jimmy greeted him with a wide smile. 'How's the Casanova of the Highlands?' he called.

'Shut yer face,' said Archie sulkily. But he joined Jimmy and ordered a pint.

'You've jist missed herself's husband,' said Jimmy. 'My, how that big fellow wass laughing about a certain skipper who had made a pass at his wife and how herself did not know what to do about it for fear of hurting the ugly wee skipper's feelings. Yon Trixie's been making a fine joke of you all around the village.'

Archie maintained a dignified silence while black murder raged in his heart.

Iain Gunn was a crofter turned farmer. He had bought the rundown old Sutherland farm over the hill from Lochdubh on Loch Coyle in 1975. Over the years, he had ploughed and seeded and worked hard, clearing more fields of old stones and glacier rocks until he had a moderately prosperous farm. His fields lay on almost the one flat piece of land in the surrounding countryside, looking more Lowland Scottish than Highland with their well-cultivated acres and herds of cattle. There was only one still unsightly area on his property. At the far corner of one of his fields was an old ramshackle two-storied ruin. He had rented a bulldozer and meant to flatten it, clear away the rubble, and then plough over the land on which the ruin stood.

He was just advancing over the fields in his rented bulldozer when he noticed a small party of women carrying banners, standing in front of the ruin. As he came nearer, he read with amazement, 'Protect Our Bats', and 'Gunn Is a Murderer'. He drove up and climbed down. He recognized Mrs Wellington, the minister's wife, Angela Brodie, and various other women from the village. The spokeswoman stepped forward. He wondered who she was and then recognized her as Lochdubh's latest incomer, Trixie Thomas.

'You shall not pass!' cried Trixie. The women behind her started marching up and down singing, 'We shall not be moved.'

He scratched his head. 'I do not have the nuclear missiles. What is all this about?'

'You have bats,' said Trixie.

'Och, you're bats yourself,' said Iain.

'No, I mean there are bats in that old ruin and bats are a protected species. You cannot touch it.'

Then Iain saw with relief a white police Land Rover, parking at the edge of the field. 'Here's Hamish,' he said, 'He'll sort you out.'

The women began chanting again as Hamish sauntered up.

'Tell these daft biddies to go away,' said Iain. 'They are after saying I cannot bulldoze that ruin because there are bats in it. Haff you ever heard the like?'

'I'm afraid they are right,' said Hamish. 'Bats are protected, Iain, and you'll need to leave that ruin alone.'

'Michty me. You mean a man cannae do whit he likes with his ain property?'

'Not when it comes to bats,' said Hamish.

Iain's face darkened with anger. 'I've a good mind to bulldoze this lot o' harpies.'

'Do you hear him, constable?' cried Trixie. 'He is threatening to kill us.'

'I didnae hear a word,' said Hamish crossly. 'But you women should be ashamed of yourselves. Yes, you too, Mrs Wellington! Somehow you heard Iain was going to bulldoze this old ruin. Well, why the h—, why on earth didn't you just write the man a letter? Behaving like silly bairns. You are a right disgrace – all of you.'

'A man as full of land greed as Iain Gunn would not have paid attention to any letter,' said Trixie.

'Now, I did hear that,' said Hamish, 'and if you want to sue her, Iain, I will be your witness. Off home with the lot of ye and try to behave like grownups. *Shoo!*'

Angela flinched. Hamish's eyes were hard.

64

How silly they all looked, she thought suddenly. Why had she come along? And Trixie had no right to say that about Iain. Crofters never liked farmers but although they occasionally made sour and jealous remarks about Iain Gunn, there was no real animosity in their hearts.

The women trailed off. 'I'll walk,' said Angela to Trixie. She had come in Trixie's old Ford van.

'Don't be silly, Angela,' said Trixie, and Angela felt she would weep if anyone ever called her silly again. 'You know how much I rely on you. We had to make a stand. Gunn wouldn't have paid any heed to a letter. Besides, I've got the minutes of the last Anti-Smoking League meeting to type out and I'm hopeless at it. Don't be cross with me. I do rely on you, Angela.' Trixie's eyes seemed very large and almost hypnotic. 'Everyone's remarked on how much you've changed lately. Why, even Mrs Wellington was saying only the other day that you were looking younger and prettier than you had done in ages.'

Angela melted. Her husband had never once in their marriage commented on her appearance until that remark about her looking like Chico Marx. Sensitive and insecure, never able to think much of herself, Angela was an easy prey for the dominant Trixie.

With a weak smile, she got in the van beside Trixie.

Iain Gunn watched them go. 'Environment-alists should be poisoned like rats,' he said.

Angela Brodie typed out the minutes while Trixie worked in the back garden and Paul sat on the wall in front of the house looking at the loch. She glanced guiltily at the clock, remembering her husband's demand for steak. The butchers would be closed quite soon. She stacked the minutes in a neat pile and ran out of the kitchen, calling to Paul to say goodbye to Trixie for her. Again, Angela felt a slight unease about Trixie, but she fought it down. Her drab life was now colourful and full of events because of Trixie. She was proud of her clean house and seemed to be on a constant high of energy and hard work. She could not go back to being the lazy, dreamy person she had been for so long. But she bought the steak.

Trixie put down her spade and walked around from the back garden to the front. She saw Priscilla Halburton-Smythe walking along the road. Trixie ran into the house and emerged a little while later with a navy-blue sweater slung over her shoulders. Ignoring her blank-eyed husband she stepped out into the road just as Priscilla was approaching. 'Good after-noon, Priscilla,' she called cheerfully.

'Good afternoon, Mrs Thomas,' said Priscilla. Her eyes fell on the sweater and a little frown marred the smooth surface of her brow. 'That looks like one of Hamish's sweaters,' she said.

Trixie lifted it from her shoulders and held it out to Priscilla. 'Would you hand it back to him?' she said, 'I'd be too embarrassed.'

'Why?' asked Priscilla, ignoring the proffered sweater.

Trixie giggled. 'Our romantic policeman's a bit soppy about me. He gave it to me to wear, you know, just like an American college kid giving his girlfriend his football sweater.'

Priscilla looked down her nose. 'Give it to him yourself,' she snapped, and walked around Trixie and off down the road.

Angela Brodie waited and waited but her husband did not return home. The cat was sleeping by the fire along with the dogs, its claws dug into the carpet in case it should be lifted up and banished to the garden again. The clock ticked slowly, marking off the time. Angela phoned the surgery but only got the answering machine referring callers to the house number. He must have been called out on an emergency, she thought, but then she had a feeling he was deliberately staying away. She tried to read but reading did not bring the old comfort. She turned on the television.

There was a party political broadcast on one channel, a sordid play on another, a wildlife programme about snakes on the third, and on the fourth, a ballet with screeching music and white-faced performers in black tights. She switched it off. She opened the cupboard under the sink and took out dusters and polish and began to clean the house all over again.

At ten o'clock, she phoned the police station. Hamish Macbeth said he would go and find the doctor. She had a feeling that Hamish knew where the doctor was.

At half past ten, the kitchen door opened and the doctor entered, or rather was helped in by Hamish. He giggled when he saw his wife and sang to the tune of Loch Lomond, 'Oh, I've just killed Trixie Thomas, the rotten harpie's dead.'

'Come to bed, doctor,' said Hamish. 'Come away. Where's the bedroom?'

'Upstairs,' said Angela weakly.

She waited, listening to the sounds as the doctor sang loudly about having killed Trixie and Hamish patiently coaxed him into bed.

She could not ever remember her husband being drunk before. But Trixie had warned her that all that smoking and junk food would cause a deterioration in him sooner or later. At the very corner of her mind was a niggling little voice accusing her of having driven her husband to drink, but she did not listen to it. Instead she tucked her sneakered feet – those gleaming, white sneakers so like Trixie's – under her on the sofa and waited for Hamish to descend.

Trixie Thomas could be harsh with her husband for his own good. The fact that Paul did not want to go to the dentist in Inverness and the fact that Trixie was determined he *should* go was all over Lochdubh by lunchtime as the couple's row on the subject had taken place in their front garden.

'Afraid o' the dentist like a wee wean,' jeered Archie Maclean who had had all his teeth pulled out at the age of twenty-one and had never had to worry about a dentist since.

Paul was eventually seen driving off in the van. At one o'clock, Mrs Kennedy, the boarder, returned to The Laurels with her sticky children to see if she could coax Trixie into making them all some sandwiches. The rain was falling steadily and the children were fractious and bored. But there was no sign of Trixie and her bedroom door was locked.

Angela Brodie turned up at two. Mrs Kennedy was cheerfully raiding the pantry. 'Mrs Thomas must be having a wee lie down,' she said. 'I cannae get a reply.'

Angela ran up the stairs and knocked on Trixie's door. Trixie had a separate room from her husband, an odd luxury in a couple who claimed they needed to rent out every available space to boarders. Angela hesitated. Then she knocked louder and called and waited. Silence.

It was a big, rambling Victorian villa. A large fly buzzed monotonously against the stained glass window on the landing. From below came the wails of the Kennedy children demanding 'mair jelly pieces' by which they meant more jam sandwiches.

Angela knew Paul had gone to Inverness to the dentist. Everyone knew that.

The silence from behind Trixie's door was uncanny.

Suddenly alarmed, Angela began to hammer at the door and shout.

Again she waited. Again that silence. The Kennedy family had fallen silent now. The fly buzzed against the glass and the rain drummed on the roof.

Angela decided to go for help. She would look a fool if they burst into that bedroom and found Trixie fast asleep. But she remembered stories in the papers of people who had not interfered for fear of looking foolish and because of that fear, someone had died.

She thought Hamish would laugh at her, but he put on his peaked cap and followed her to The Laurels. His face was set and grim. He tried to tell himself his feeling of foreboding was the weather. The midges danced through the raindrops, stinging his face and he automatically fished in his pocket for his stick of repellent.

He walked up the stairs past the Kennedy family who were gathered at the foot. The children were strangely silent, their jam-covered faces turned upwards.

He went up to Trixie's room and hammered on the door. Then he tilted his head on one side and listened to the quality of the silence.

'Stand back,' he said curtly to Angela.

He kicked at the lock with all his might and there came a splintering sound and the door burst open.

Trixie Thomas lay half across the bed, her hair spilled over her face. He gently put back her hair and looked down at her contorted face and then he felt her pulse.

'Get your husband here,' he said over his shoulder.

'Is she . . .?' Angela put her hands up to her mouth.

'Yes. But get him anyway.'

Angela ran down the stairs and along the waterfront towards the surgery. Rain water poured down her face like the tears she could not yet shed.

The receptionist called something as she ran past and burst into the consulting room.

'Come quickly,' Angela called.

Dr Brodie was examining Mrs Wellington's bared bosom with a stethoscope. Angela

71

reflected wildly that she had never seen such enormous breasts before.

'Mrs Brodie!' screeched the outraged minister's wife, seizing a brassiere the size of a hammock.

'It's Trixie. She's dead,' said Angela, and then the tears came and great suffocating sobs.

'Dear me. Dear me,' said Mrs Wellington, encasing her girth rapidly in underwear and Harris tweed.

Dr Brodie seized his bag and ran out of the surgery to his car. Hamish was waiting for him in Trixie's bedroom. 'Don't move the body if you can,' he said when he saw the doctor. 'I'll have a look around outside.'

The doctor spent only a short time in the room. Hamish was coming along the corridor when Dr Brodie emerged outside.

'I'll just write the death certificate,' said the doctor. 'Heart attack. No doubt about it.'

Hamish's eyes narrowed and he said quietly, 'Go back in there and try again. It's case of poisoning, if ever I saw one.

'It's murder, doctor. Pure and straightforward murder!'

Chapter Four

The very pink of perfection.
– Oliver Goldsmith

The day after Trixie's death was perfect. The clouds rolled back and the sun blazed down on a glittering, wet landscape. Bees hummed among the roses tumbling over the police station door as Hamish Macbeth waited for news from the laboratory in Strathbane.

He had to ask a lot of questions – starting with Dr Brodie. Why had the doctor been so keen to diagnose a heart attack? But there was always the slim hope in Hamish's mind that somehow it would turn out to be food poisoning.

He had reported his suspicions to Mr Daviot. That gentleman had finished his holiday and had been packing to leave when Hamish had arrived at the hotel. To Hamish's surprise, he treated the news of Trixie's death lightly. Hamish did not know that because of Hamish's addled behaviour at the Halburton-Smythe dinner party, the superintendent had swung round to Blair's view of the village constable, which was that Macbeth had a slate missing.

But Mr Daviot had called at The Laurels, been satisfied that the forensic boys had taken away everything possible from the kitchen for analysis, and then had driven off.

Hamish still shuddered when he remembered the ordeal of breaking the news to Paul Thomas. The big man had seemed to crumple up and shrivel inside his clothes. Dr Brodie had given him a sedative. Now all Trixie's fan club were in attendance on the bereaved husband.

The arrival of Detective Chief Inspector Blair was imminent, but surely there would not be the hordes of press that had attended the last two murders in Lochdubh ... if it should prove to be murder. The murder of a house-wife in the Highlands would be of interest only to the local press.

He went out into the front garden carrying a battered old deck chair and stretched out in the sun. Why had Trixie had such a hold over the women of Lochdubh? he wondered. She had, of course, quite a powerful personality. Then the village women themselves were mostly of the old school, that is, they were housewives rather than wage earners. There was no cinema in Lochdubh, no theatre, no discos, or parties. The wonder of television had long worn off. Trixie, Hamish decided, had given them all a purpose. They were still housewives in an age that had been taught to despise housewives. The days of the enormous families had gone. Time, Hamish supposed, must lie heavily on a woman's hands. It was all right for him to be lazy and stretch out in the sun when he had the chance. Apart from his police work, he had his garden, his sheep, and his hens to look after. The only thing which made a demand on his affections was Towser. He reached down and scratched the dog behind the ears. Even when their husbands died, he mused, the women of Lochdubh did not promptly travel to Inverness or Strathbane looking for work. Most of them had never gone out to work in their lives, having got married as soon as they left school. Of course a lot of them worked very hard, doing most of the gardening and, if the husband had a croft, an equal share of the work load. But there were the long winter months where everything ground to a halt and they were not paid for their labours. Anything they did was part of their wifely duties.

A lot of the local men, he knew, married not out of love but because their mothers had died or because they wanted a home of their own with someone to cook the meals and iron the shirts.

Priscilla had been right about Angela Brodie. She had the soul of an academic. Good intelligence there and absolutely no common-sense whatsoever. Incapable of judging character. Hamish fervently hoped for both the Brodies' sakes that Angela would revert back to her old self. But would she? She had become accustomed to interests outside her books.

Hamish rose and ambled into the office and searched through a file of phone numbers that he had jotted down from time to time in the hope that they would prove useful. At last he found what he wanted. He phoned the Open University in Milton Keynes and said he was phoning for a Mrs Brodie who was interested in taking a science degree and would they send her the necessary papers? When he put down the phone, he had a feeling of satisfaction. Studying for a degree at home would be just the thing for Angela Brodie and a science degree would give her something difficult and practical to work on. The Open University enabled men and women to work for University degrees at home.

He returned to his deck chair.

He lay back and closed his eyes and listened to the sounds of the village, the chugging of a donkey engine on a boat out on the loch, snatches of song from a radio, the harsh scream of the wheeling seagulls, and the lazy drone of a car winding its way through the hills behind. It was a pity, he thought, that all the skylarks seemed to have gone. He could remember them in his youth, the very sound of summer, climbing to the heavens and sending down a cascade of glorious sound. No one could remain an atheist with larks around, he thought dreamily.

'Wouldnae that make ye sick,' said a harsh voice, and a shadow fell across him.

Hamish opened his eyes and struggled up. Blocking out the sun was the square bulk of Detective Chief Inspector Blair. Standing behind him were his two sidekicks, Detectives Jimmy Anderson and Harry MacNab.

Blair was in a bad temper. Daviot had said the prices at the Lochdubh Hotel were much too high and so Blair and his team must commute daily from Strathbane, a drive of an hour and a half over twisting Highland roads. The sight of Hamish lounging at his ease in the sun did nothing to help his temper.

'We've jist had the lab report,' said Blair. 'Thon Thomas woman was poisoned wi' arsenic.'

'Arsenic!' Hamish got to his feet. 'What from? Rat poison?'

'Straight arsenic as far as I know,' said Blair.

'What were the contents of the stomach?'

'Curry, rice, bread and cake. They think it was probably in the curry.'

Hamish hesitated. It was his duty to tell Blair about the odd behaviour of the doctor. He liked Dr Brodie and did not like to think of him being bullied by Blair. On the other hand, Dr Brodie was well able to take care of himself.

Perhaps the best thing was to suggest that he, Hamish, should interview the doctor.

'I'd better tell you about this,' said Hamish. 'When Dr Brodie first examined the body, he was going to sign a death certificate saying she had died of a heart attack. I stopped him doing that.'

'Whit!' Blair's piggy eyes gleamed.

'So maybe I had better go along to the surgery and see him,' said Hamish.

'Listen, laddie, you jist go aboot your rural duties,' said Blair with a fat grin. 'But I tell ye what – I'll let ye in on the case. Go down to Inverness tomorrow and interview that dentist Paul Thomas went to see.'

'One phone call to Inverness police could get that done now,' said Hamish with surprise.

'Do as you're told,' snapped Blair. He marched off, a squat figure, sweating in a heavy tweed suit, and followed by his two detectives.

Hamish sighed. He may as well just look forward to a pleasant day in Inverness. Let Blair solve this one. He did not care very much who had murdered Trixie.

But as he looked along the road, he could see the slumped figure of Paul Thomas, sitting on his garden wall. Calling to Towser, Hamish went along to talk to him.

But before he could reach him, he was way-laid by the Glasgow woman, Mrs Kennedy. 'How long are we going to have to stay here?'

she complained. 'I want tae get the wee yins back to Glasgow.'

'Should be a few more days,' said Hamish.

'But this wis supposed to be a holiday and I'm having to dae all the cooking, and buy the food, for the polis took everything out of the kitchen. I telt Mr Thomas he wasnae getting any money from me.' She was a fat, sloppy woman wearing a print apron over a mud-coloured dress and carpet slippers on her swollen feet. The children all looked about six years old, but they could hardly all be the same age. They had white pinched faces and old, old eyes: three boys called Elvis, Clarke and Gregory and a girl called Susan.

Hamish promised to see what he could do about letting them go and then went on to speak to Paul. Paul looked at him with dull eyes.

'Terrible business,' said Hamish gently.

Paul's eyes filled with tears. 'Who could have done such a thing? Everybody loved her.'

'This is a small village and we'll soon find out who did it,' said Hamish soothingly.

Paul put his hands on Hamish's shoulders. 'You find out,' he said. 'Don't leave it to that fool, Blair.'

'I promise,' said Hamish gently. 'Is anyone with you?'

'People have been very kind.' Tears ran down Paul's cheeks and he wiped them away with his sleeve.

79

'I met Mrs Kennedy, but where's your other boarder?'

'Oh, him? He's about somewhere.'

'Staying a long time, isn't he? What does he do for a living.'

'He's a writer. Hammering at that type-writer of his day and night.'

'What's his name? I've forgotten.'

'John Parker.'

'Ah, yes. Maybe I'll have a word with him. Hadn't you better go and lie down? You look awful.'

'I can't lie down.' Paul's face twisted with distress. 'Every time I close my eyes, I see her dead face.'

'Well, maybe you'd better tire yourself out. You still doing the garden?'

'I was, but Trixie took over and she seemed to be better at it than me and so . . .'

'Well, let's go around and have a look,' said Hamish.

The two men walked around to the back garden. 'Hasn't been touched for a bit,' said Hamish. 'Look at the weeds. Why don't you get started again?'

Paul nodded dumbly and started to weed between the rows of vegetables.

Hamish heard a car arriving and left him and walked around the front. John Parker, the writer, was just getting out.

'Bad business,' he said when he saw Hamish.

'Has the CID asked you about your movements on the day of the murder yet?' asked Hamish.

'Not yet.'

'They'll be along shortly. So you're a writer, are you? I'm trying to remember if I've seen the name John Parker on the bookshelves.'

'Well, you won't. I write under the name of Brett Saddler.'

'You're Brett Saddler? The man who writes the Westerns?'

'That's me,' said John with a faint smile.

'I always thought Brett Saddler was an American.'

'I've always liked Westerns,' said John. 'Must have seen about every Western movie ever made. I give them the good old-fashioned stuff. As a matter of fact, Westerns have made a come-back. I sold the film rights of my last one, which is why I'm able to take this long holiday.'

'My! You must be a millionaire.'

'Far from it,' said John. 'I got twenty-five thousand dollars, and by the time you take agent's fees off that, and British tax, there isn't all that much left. If you want to know where I was when Trixie died, I was off driving up in the hills. I like it up there. So quiet.'

'Anyone see you?'

'No, I didn't meet a soul,' he said cheerfully.

'Do you know if anyone else had any of that curry she had been eating?'

'I shouldn't think so. She must have had it for lunch. The Kennedys had sandwiches and Mrs Kennedy is of the opinion that curry is foreign muck. I wasn't here and Paul was in Inverness.'

'Did the forensic boys find any pot that had been used to cook the curry?'

'No, everything in the kitchen had been scrubbed clean. Trixie was the perfect house-wife.'

'Did you know her before?'

'No. Now I've got to get back to my writing.' He gave a lethargic wave of his hand and went into the house.

Hamish then thought of Archie Maclean, who had been seen holding hands with Trixie. It had been all over Lochdubh. Had Mrs Maclean known?

He was walking back along the waterfront when he saw Priscilla's Volvo approaching at a slow pace. He felt in his bones that for some reason she was going to drive right past him so he stood in the middle of the road and held up his hand.

'What is it, copper?' asked Priscilla. 'You can hardly accuse me of speeding.'

'Just wanted a chat.'

'I'm a bit busy.'

'Now, now, what *iss* the matter? You have eyes like the North Sea.'

Priscilla stared straight ahead, her hands

resting on the wheel. She was angry with Hamish over Trixie's tale about that sweater. Although she knew Trixie must have been lying, she could not help remembering old stories about Hamish's various flirtations. Priscilla was completely unaware that Hamish Macbeth was attracted to her. She knew he liked her but thought he looked on her sometimes as being rather young and silly.

When Priscilla did not reply, Hamish said, 'Someone has been saying something to put your back up. It cannot be your father, for he's said about everything there is to say. So who could it be?'

'I feel you made a bit of a fool of yourself over Trixie.'

'And me the only person in Lochdubh who couldn't stand the female,' said Hamish, 'apart from Brodie, that is.'

'I met her wearing one of your old sweaters,' said Priscilla. 'She said you gave it to her and made a pass at her or something.'

'I neffer gave her anything,' said Hamish in amazement. He frowned and then said, 'I have it. She went out driving with your father and your father must have told her about his worries that you might run off with the local bobby. She came round to me and said she was going to the toilet and she was away for a long time and then she left by the front. She must have picked up my sweater just to annoy you.'

He leaned on the car. 'I am very flattered it did annoy you.'

'It only annoyed me because I would not like to see any friend of mine making a fool of himself over such a woman,' said Priscilla. 'I've got to go, Hamish. I'm expected at home.'

'What about dropping in tomorrow for a chat?' asked Hamish.

'I can't. I'm taking this car over to Golspie for its annual Ministry of Transport check tomorrow – I don't trust any other garage – and then taking the train to Inverness to do some shopping for mother.'

'I'm going to Inverness myself,' said Hamish. 'What time will your train get in?'

'Twelve-thirty.'

'What if I meet you at the station and then we can go for lunch and I'll drive you back.' Hamish waited anxiously.

'All right,' said Priscilla. 'Now do get out of the way.'

Hamish stood back and watched her go with a grin on his face.

Then he decided to go and call on Mrs Maclean. Mrs Maclean had not been one of the women at the bat demonstration. Trixie's hold had been on the middle-class and lower-middle-class women who had kitchens full of labour-saving devices and therefore more time on their hands.

Mrs Maclean was down on her knees, scrubbing her stone-flagged kitchen floor with ammonia. Not for her the easy way with mop and up-to-date cleanser.

The radio was blaring out Scottish country dance music. He called to her, but she didn't hear him so he switched off the radio and she looked up.

'What do you want, you glaiket loon?' she said, wringing the floor cloth savagely and throwing it into the bucket.

Hamish sighed. The trouble with being a policeman in a small, normally law-abiding village was that you did not strike fear or terror into the heart of anyone.

'I'm making enquiries into the death of Trixie Thomas,' he said.

'Why?' Mrs Maclean sat back on her heels. 'That wumman's better off dead.'

'Maybe,' he said. 'But since yourself had no reason to like her, you are one of my suspects.' He looked at her sternly, but she gave a contemptuous snort.

'She made a fool o' that silly man o' mine. He thought she fancied him when all that moocher wanted was a bit o' free fish. Take the sugar out o' your tea, that one would. It's my opinion the Thomases had money enough, but they was always talking about being hard up and scrounging everything they could get. The minister's wife goes around saying Mrs Thomas was the perfect housewife. She was perfect when it came to getting other people to do the work for her. Thae women like Mrs

Wellington and that Mrs Brodie haven't enough to do. Microwaves and washing machines. A disgrace I call it.'

A strong smell of bleach rose from a huge copper pot of sheets on the wood burning stove. Mrs Maclean was famous for her 'whites', boiling everything and hanging it over the bushes in the garden to bleach further on a sunny day. Perhaps that was why Archie's Maclean's clothes always looked too tight for him, reflected Hamish. She probably boiled his suits.

'Well, you'll have the detectives around soon asking you questions as well,' said Hamish. 'They'll want to know where you were when she was murdered.'

Mrs Maclean picked up the scrubbing brush again and scrubbed an area of already clean floor. 'They can ask away,' she said, 'for I was right here all day, and my neighbours all saw me coming and going between the house and the garden.'

'And Archie?'

'Himself was down at the nets.'

Hamish all at once remembered Dr Brodie singing about Trixie being dead and felt cold. That was something he should have told Blair as well. Damn Blair.

'Anyway,' said Mrs Maclean, picking out the floor cloth and wringing it out and wiping the wet floor, 'you'll probably find it was that husband o' hers what did it.'

'He was in Inverness at the dentist.'

Mrs Maclean sniffed. 'So *he* says.'

When Hamish left by the garden gate, he heard a burst of music. Mrs Maclean had turned on the radio again.

He remembered his promise to Paul. Somewhere in Lochdubh, there was a murderer. But it was hard to think such a thing had happened. The sun beat down on a perfect scene. The eighteenth-century cottages along the waterfront gleamed white. Roses scented the air and the still waters of the loch reflected the hills and woods and the gaily painted hulls of the fishing boats.

Trixie had gone and something nasty in the atmosphere had gone with her. And yet she had not been an evil woman. And the women of Lochdubh would have got wise to her in time.

He saw Blair and his two detectives driving out of the village and made his way to the doctor's surgery.

Dr Brodie said he would see Hamish. 'Quiet day,' he said when Hamish walked into the consulting room. 'Monday's the busy day when they all come in with their bad backs. It's the Highland disease. Every Monday morning, a bad back strikes them and they want a line so they do not have to go to work.'

'How did you get on with Blair?' asked Hamish.

'He tried to bully me. Threatened to arrest me. You told him about me diagnosing a heart attack.'

'I had to,' said Hamish quietly. 'Why did you do that?'

'As I told that fat lump, it looked like a heart attack to me.'

'Oh, come on, John,' said Hamish, exasperated. 'It looked like nothing o' the kind. Spit out the truth, man. It looked bad. You had been drunk out your skull the night before and singing about how you had killed Trixie. Did you know her real name was Alexandra?'

'Yes. But she's the sort of woman – she was the sort of woman – who would think a name like Trixie cute. Well, Hamish, I'll tell you but don't tell Blair unless you think it necessary. I knew she had been poisoned. You had told me Paul Thomas was in Inverness but it went right out of my head. I thought maybe he had done it. I was glad she was dead. I didn't want anyone to get the blame. I lost my head. Can you blame me? My wife's a changed woman. I can't remember the last time I saw her in a skirt and heels. I've been living with a carbon copy of Trixie – smocks and jeans and those bloody sneakers squeaking over the floorboards.'

'She should be all right now,' said Hamish awkwardly.

'Oh, no, Trixie's memory must not die. Angela's taken over the bird thing and the smoking thing and the clean up of Lochdubh rubbish. Either I eat salads or eat out. She's hard as nails.'

'Shock, maybe. Look, women of your wife's age don't change for life. You'll have her back soon. Just go along with it for a bit.'

'She thinks I murdered Trixie.'

'Don't be daft.'

'It's a fact. I see her watching me with those hard, hard eyes. She's moved her bed into the spare room. If you find out who did it, let me know first, Hamish. I want to shake that man by the hand.'

'It might be a woman,' said Hamish.

Dr Brodie leaned back in his chair and lit a cigarette. 'It might at that,' he said slowly.

Hamish had imagined his visit to Inverness would prove to be blessed with another sunny day. But to his annoyance, the weather had turned dark and rainy.

He called on the dentist, a Mr Jones, who was justifiably annoyed at his call, having already been interviewed by the Inverness police. Hamish was not surprised. He knew Blair had sent him to Inverness to get him out of the way.

'You are such an important witness, Mr Jones,' he said, 'that I am afraid you have to be questioned all over again. I will not be taking up much of your time.'

'Oh, well,' said the dentist, mollified. 'There's not much to tell. What a baby that man was. He had a bad toothache because one of his back teeth was rotten. The root was all right so I said I would drill it and put in a filling. He started to shake and tremble and begged me to pull it out. Wouldn't take no for an answer. Insisted on having gas. When he came round, I showed him his X-rays and said he needed a lot of work done and then he really panicked. He staggered out of the chair and ran for the door. It's a good thing I'd got his National Health number before I'd started or I would have ended up doing that extraction for free. He should have rested a bit till the effects of the gas wore off.'

A bluebottle landed on the dentist's white coat and he brushed it off with a shudder. 'I've never seen so many flies as we've had this summer,' said Mr Jones. 'But the air's so warm and clammy, I can't keep the windows closed.'

Hamish put away his notebook and headed for the station. He would just be in time to meet Priscilla's train.

He put all thoughts of the case from his mind and concentrated on the simple pleasure of waiting for her to arrive. He found he was imagining a sort of *Brief Encounter* situations. She would run towards him through the steam, her fair hair bobbing on her shoulders, and throw herself into his arms. But the days of steam trains were long over. He did not want to abandon one bit of his rosy fantasy. So the steam remained. Rain thudded down on the station roof and the restless seagulls of Inverness called overhead.

Twelve-thirty came and went and there was no sign of the train. He went up to the information kiosk but there was no one there. He went into the Travel Centre where he was told the train would be half an hour late due to signal failure. He returned to the platform and waited and again that dream Priscilla endlessly ran towards him.

After three quarters of an hour, he returned to the Travel Centre. He was again told the story about signal failure and that the train should be in any minute. The loudspeaker in the station burst into song. It was one of those Scottish songs written to the beat of a Scottish waltz and sung through the nose.

'Oh, there's the purple o' the heather,
And the ships aboot the bay,
And it's there that I would wander,
At the kelosing hoff the day,'

sang the voice and the rain fell harder on the roof and the wheeling seagulls screamed louder as if to compete with the singer.

Hamish went back to the Travel Centre with that feeling of impotence that assails the average Britisher in dealing with British Rail. A young man in a tartan jacket and with a sulky 'get lost' expression on his face eventually phoned the station manager's office after Hamish had told him quietly what he would do to him if he didn't look more willing. There was a broken rail outside Inverness, said the young man. But the train would be moving soon.

Back again went Hamish. At two-fifteen, the train crawled into the platform.

He waited by the barrier.

He nearly missed her. She was walking with her head down, her hair covered by a depressing rain hat.

'Priscilla!' he called.

She swung round. 'Oh, there you are,' she said coolly. 'Rotten train. I'm starving. Where are we going?'

Hamish blinked at her. He had been dreaming so long of that passionate arrival that he had forgotten to think about where to take her.

'We could try the Caledonian Hotel,' he said.

They walked in silence along to the hotel that overlooks the River Ness to find that it stopped serving lunches at two. Hamish found a phone box and tried several other places to find they had stopped serving lunch at two as well.

'Hamish, let's just pick somewhere cheap and easy,' said Priscilla. Water was dripping from the brim of her hat on to her nose.

Hamish looked around desperately. There was a cheap-looking restaurant called the

Admiral's Nook. The bow window was festooned with fishing nets.

'This'll do,' he said.

They went inside and sat at a crumby table.

Hamish looked at the menu. There was a wide choice. Waitresses were standing in a group at the back of the restaurant, talking. He waved his hand. Several blank stares were directed towards him and then they all went on talking again.

'Pick out what you want,' said Hamish.

'What about spaghetti bolognaise?' said Priscilla. 'These places usually have a Scottish-Italian cook.'

'All right.' Hamish approached the waitresses. 'Two plates of spaghetti bolognaise,' he ordered. They all looked at him as if he had said several obscene words and then one peeled off from the group and headed for the kitchen.

Hamish returned to the table. He wondered if Priscilla was thinking of that John Burlington, who would probably have organized things better.

The waitress approached with two plates piled high with spaghetti and topped with a sort of grey sludge. Her hands were covered in scabs.

'Where's the parmesan cheese?' asked Hamish faint but pursuing.

'Whit?'

'Parmesan cheese,' said Priscilla in icy tones.

'We dinnae hae any o' that,' said the waitress triumphantly.

'Well, brush the crumbs off the table,' said Hamish crossly. She slouched off and did not return.

'This smells like feet,' said Priscilla. 'I daren't eat it.'

'Come away,' said Hamish, putting down his fork. 'This damn place reeks of salmonella. No, I'm not calling for the bill, nor am I going to protest. It would take all day.' He checked the menu for the price and left several Scottish pound notes on the table and marched Priscilla outside.

'Where now?' asked Priscilla bleakly.

'Follow me,' said Hamish grimly. He led her to where his Land Rover was parked. 'Stay there,' he said, holding open the door for her.

He came back after some time carrying two packets of fish and chips, a bottle of wine, a bottle of mineral water, two glasses, and a corkscrew.

'The wine's for you,' he said, uncorking it.

'Food at last,' said Priscilla.

They ate in a contented silence. 'Sorry I was so grumpy,' said Priscilla. 'How did you get on?'

'Oh, Thomas was at that dentist all right.'

'But it doesn't mean he didn't do it,' said Priscilla.

'Why?'

'He could have put the arsenic in something he knew she would eat before he left.'

'They've got everything out of the kitchen and there's not a smell of arsenic anywhere. Except the curry. Can't find any of that.'

'Curry? Oh, I know about the curry,' said Priscilla. 'She made some for herself and gave the rest to Mrs Wellington for the minister's supper.'

Hamish realized he was looking at her with his mouth open. 'Better get back,' he said. 'If she hasn't eaten it, it might still be in her fridge. No better still, wait here and I'll phone.'

He returned after ten minutes, his face triumphant. 'She didn't touch the curry. Trixie took some for herself out of the pot and gave the rest in the pot to Mrs Wellington. She's still got it. I've phoned Blair.'

'I'd better do that shopping for mother,' said Priscilla. 'Do you want to wait here?'

'Yes, how long will you be?'

'About an hour.'

Hamish sat in the station car park and thought about the case. But after almost an hour was up, he kept glancing in his rearview mirror to see if there was any sign of Priscilla coming back.

And that was when he saw a car just leaving the car park. On the roof rack was a chair covered in transparent plastic sheeting. He was sure he recognized that chair. He started up the engine, swung the Land Rover around, and started off in pursuit.

The car in front was travelling very fast. It went around the roundabout and headed out on the A9 towards Perth. Hamish put on the siren but the car in front only seemed to go faster.

He caught up with it twenty miles out on the Perth road and signalled to the driver to halt. The driver, a small, ferrety, red-haired man rolled down the window and the reason why he had not heard the police siren became apparent as a blast of sound from his tape deck struck Hamish like a blow.

'What is it?' said the man crossly.

'You were doing over the limit for a start,' said Hamish. 'Where did you get that chair?'

'At the auction rooms in Inverness. I'm a dealer.' He handed over a grimy business card.

'Get out and let's have a look at it and I'll maybe forget about the speeding.'

'I'll just lift up a corner of the sheeting,' said the dealer, whose name was Henderson. 'Don't want it to get wet.'

Hamish peered under the plastic. It was the Brodies' chair that he had last seen when Trixie had been carrying it along the road.

'How much did you pay for it?' asked Hamish.

'A hundred and fifty.'

Hamish whistled. 'And where are you taking it?'

'Down to London eventually. I've got several more auctions to go to. Get a better price for it there. It's a Victorian nursing chair. Good condition. Look at the bead work.'

'Do you know where it came from?'

'Auctioneer said some knocker from the north brought it in.'

'Knocker?'

'One of those women that goes around houses spotting antiques where the owners don't know the value. Usually offers them a fiver for something worth a few hundred.'

'Or gets it for nothing,' said Hamish, half to himself. Aloud he said, 'I won't be booking you this time, Mr Henderson, but go carefully. I might be getting in touch with you.'

'It isn't stolen, is it?' asked the dealer anxiously.

'No, but don't sell it for another week. It may be connected with a murder.'

Hamish drove back. The rain was coming down heavier than ever. He remembered Priscilla and put his foot down on the accelerator.

She was not in the car park. He went into the station and looked around. No Priscilla. He looked at the indicator board and saw a train for the north was just leaving. He ran to the platform in time to see the back of it disappearing around the curve of the track.

So much for *Brief Encounter*, he thought miserably.

He drove to the auction rooms and found

that Trixie had put the chair in for sale along with some other pieces of furniture and china ornaments.

'We had an auction last evening,' said the auctioneer. 'I was about to send Mrs Thomas her cheque.'

'How much?'

'Nearly a thousand pounds. She could have got a lot more in London but I wasn't about to tell her that.'

Hamish told him to hold the cheque until they found out if Trixie had left a will.

He drove through the slashing rain and winding roads until he reached the police station at Lochdubh.

He phoned Tommel Castle and asked for Priscilla without remembering to disguise his voice. 'Miss Halburton-Smythe is not here,' said Jenkins.

Hamish wondered whether she was still waiting in Inverness.

He phoned the castle again and, disguising his voice, stated he was John Burlington. This time Priscilla answered the phone.

'Oh, it's you, Hamish,' she said in a flat voice.

'I'm awfully sorry, Priscilla,' said Hamish. He told her about the chair.

'That's all right,' said Priscilla, although her voice sounded distant. 'There's a little bit of information that might interest you. Jessie, the maid, says she saw Trixie going over to the seer's at Coyle. You could ask him what he told her.'

When Hamish put down the phone, he thought about going over to the seer's that evening, but decided to leave it till the morning. Angus Macdonald, the seer, had built up a reputation for being able to predict the future. Hamish thought he was an old fraud, but the local people were proud of him and believed every word he said. On the other hand, it would be unlike Trixie to go alone. She probably had taken some of her acolytes with her. He asked Angela Brodie, Mrs Wellington, and several others but they knew nothing about it. He asked Mrs Kennedy and the boarder, John Carter, and then Paul, without success.

Then he remembered that Colonel Halburton-Smythe had said he was going to take Trixie over to Mrs Haggerty's old cottage. He looked at his watch. They would be finishing dinner at the castle and so the colonel could not accuse him of scrounging and perhaps he could talk to Priscilla and apologize again for having left her in Inverness.

But the colonel was determined Hamish was not going to be allowed anywhere near his daughter.

He told Hamish curtly that Trixie had taken several bits and pieces of old furniture.

'I'd better go and look at the place,' said Hamish, 'if that's all right with you.'

'I suppose I'd better let you have the key,' said the colonel, 'but I can't see what it's got to do with a murder investigation.'

'I'll look anyway,' said Hamish. 'She sold some of that furniture and a chair that Angela Brodie gave her for nearly a thousand pounds at the auction in Inverness.'

'I find that hard to believe,' blustered the colonel. 'Fine woman, she was. Very womanly, if you know what I mean. That lout of a husband probably sold the stuff when he was down at the dentist's. She would not have tricked me.'

'Maybe. Let me have the key anyway. Did she say anything about going over to Angus Macdonald?'

'Not that I remember. I hope that's an end to your questions, Macbeth. If I thought for one moment you suspected me of this murder, I would report you to your superiors.'

Hamish sadly left the castle. Priscilla must know he had been visiting for the servants would have told her. But there was no sign of her. The castle door slammed behind him, a bleak finality in the sound. He was disgusted with himself. He thought of his fevered fantasies at the station, of the way that kiss had started him dreaming again, and put Priscilla Halburton-Smythe firmly from his mind.

But there seemed to be a great black emptiness there for she had occupied his thoughts for so long.

Chapter Five

I know of no way of judging the future but by the past.
— Patrick Henry

Hamish was just moving out of the police station in the Land Rover in the morning when Blair appeared, holding up a beefy hand.

'I hear ye're going to consult the oracle,' he said with a grin.

'Meaning what?'

'It's all over the village that Angus Macdonald is going tae solve the case by looking at his crystal balls.'

'Want to go yourself?' asked Hamish.

'I've got mair to dae with ma time. Typed out your report frae the dentist?'

'Why bother?' said Hamish laconically. 'It's the same stuff you got from the police in Inverness. But there's something you should know.' He told Blair about the dealer.

'Bugger it,' said Blair. 'That complicates

things. She'd probably made off with someone's family heirloom.'

'You should ask Halburton-Smythe,' said Hamish maliciously. 'He was driving her around while she looked for antiques.'

Blair's face darkened. The Daviots had been bragging about their dinner at the castle and he had no desire to run foul of the new super by putting the colonel's back up. 'Aye, well, I might send Anderson up. This is the devil of a case. There was nae arsenic in that curry. Must hae been in something else.'

Towser, who was sitting beside Hamish, growled softly.

'You look right daft with that mongrel beside you,' sneered Blair.

'This is a highly trained police dog,' said Hamish, 'and I've already been offered five hundred pounds for him.'

Blair's mouth dropped in surprise as Hamish drove off.

'It wasn't really a lie,' Hamish told Towser. 'If they had any sense in this place, I'm sure they would have given me an offer for you.' Towser lolled his tongue and put a large affectionate paw on Hamish's knee.

'Should be a woman's hand on my knee,' said Hamish, 'and not a mangy dog like yourself.'

The seer lived in a small white-washed cottage on the top of a round green hill with a winding path leading up to it. It looked like a child's drawing. Hamish parked his vehicle at the foot of the path and began to walk up. Black storm clouds rolled across the heavens and the wind roared through a pylon over-head with a dismal shriek. At least the wind is keeping away the flies and midges, thought Hamish, leaning against its force as he walked towards the cottage. A thin column of grey smoke from one of the cottage's chimneys was being whipped and shredded by the wind.

Angus Macdonald was a tall, thin man in his sixties. He had a thick head of white hair and a craggy face with an enormous beak of a nose. His eyes were very pale grey.

He opened the door as Hamish reached it. 'So ye've come at last,' he said. 'I knew you'd be by. Cannae solve the case?'

'And I suppose you can,' said Hamish, following the seer into his small kitchen-cum-living room.

'Aye, maybe, maybe,' said Angus. 'Whit have ye brought me?'

'Nothing. What did you want? Your palm crossed with silver?'

'Folks aye bring me something. A bit o' salmon, or a piece of venison or a homemade cake.'

'I am here to ask you to tell me as an officer of the law what you know about Trixie Thomas.'

'She's dead,' said the seer and cackled with laughter.

'When she came to see you, what did you tell her?'

Angus lifted a black kettle from its chain over the open fire and took it over to the sink and filled it with water and then hung it back on the hook. 'I've a bad memory these days,' he said. 'Seems tae me that there's nothing like a wee dram for bringing it to life.'

'I haven't brought any whisky with me,' said Hamish crossly.

The seer turned from the fire and bent a penetrating gaze on Hamish. 'She'll never marry you,' he said.

The Highland part of Hamish repressed a superstitious shudder. The policeman part decided to be diplomatic.

'Look, you auld scunner,' he said, 'I'll be back in a bit with a dram. You'd better get your brains working by then.'

Angus smiled when Hamish had left and then set about making a pot of tea. The wind howled and screeched about his cottage like a banshee. He could hear nothing but the fury of the wind. He hoped Hamish would be back soon with that whisky. The wind depressed him. It seemed like a live thing, some monster howling about his cottage, seeking a way in.

It was probably playing havoc with his garden at the back. He put the teapot on the hearth beside the fire and then opened the back door. His raspberry canes were flattened and the door of his garden shed was swinging wildly on its hinges. He went out into the small garden and shut the shed door and wedged a brick against it.

A fitful gleam of watery sunlight struck through the clouds as he turned around and shone on something lying beside his back door. He went and looked down. A full bottle of whisky.

He grinned. Just like devious Hamish Macbeth. Leaving the whisky and hoping he'd get well oiled before the constable came back to ask his questions.

He carried the bottle inside. Time to switch on the television and watch the long-range forecast. People were always amazed at his ability to predict the weather so accurately although they watched the same programme themselves. He settled down in his battered armchair by the fire and poured himself a glass of whisky, noticing that the top had already been opened. 'Decided to have a dram himself and thought the better of it,' reflected Angus with amusement.

The wind increased in force and shrieked and battered at his cottage like a maniac. As he raised his glass to his lips, the room whirled away and he suddenly saw his long dead mother. She was looking surprised and delighted, the way she had looked when he had unexpectedly come home on leave during the war. And then the vision faded. He sat very still and then put the glass down on the floor beside him with a shaking hand.

As a youth, he had been sure he had been gifted with the second sight, as that ability to see into the future is called in the Highlands. He had had it during the war. He had seen in his mind's eye his friend getting shot by the Germans and sure enough that's exactly what had happened. He had gradually built up the reputation of a seer. The gift had never come back, but he had found it easy to impress the locals as he knew all about them anyway and listened to every bit of gossip.

He was sitting, staring into space, when Hamish came back.

'Here's your whisky,' said Hamish, holding up a half bottle. 'Why, you greedy auld pig, you've got a whole bottle there.'

'It's death,' said the seer in a thin voice. 'Oh, tak' it away, Hamish. I saw death in it.'

He was white and trembling.

'Where did you get it from?' asked Hamish sharply.

'It was outside the kitchen door – at the back. People aye leave me things, you know that, Hamish. I didnae hear anyone because o' that damn wind.'

'And what stopped ye?' asked Hamish, looking at him intently.

Angus shook his head as if to clear it. 'I saw my mither,' he said. 'She was standing by the door and she looked surprised tae see me as if I'd jist crossed over tae the other side.'

'And ye hadn't been drinking anything before that?' asked Hamish cynically.

'No, man, no. I swear it.'

Hamish took out a clean handkerchief and lifted the bottle of whisky. 'Have you a bit o' kitchen paper or something so I can take the glass as well?' he asked.

Angus nodded in the direction of the sink where there was a roll of kitchen paper standing on the draining board.

'I'll just be off,' said Hamish, tenderly carrying both glass and bottle.

'Dinnae leave me,' wailed Angus, getting to his feet.

'Aye, I suppose ye'd better come with me to Blair, although what he's going to make of this, I shudder to think.'

Blair was in the police station office when Hamish returned with the seer. The police station, like most of the houses in Lochdubh, was hardly ever locked.

'I know you're not staying at the hotel,' said Hamish crossly, 'but I thought Johnson had given you the free use of a room.'

'Aye, well I jist happened to be passing and needed tae use the phone. Who's he? And whit are ye daein' stinking o' whisky?' Hamish was carefully carrying a glass of whisky and the bottle he had taken from Angus.

Hamish and the seer sat down and Hamish in a colourless voice recounted Angus's vision.

Blair laughed and laughed, slapping his knees in delight. 'Daviot's arrived from Strathbane. He's along at the hotel now tae see how the investigation's going on. Wait till he hears aboot this?'

Blair gleefully picked up the phone and started to dial. If ever the superintendent needed extra proof that Hamish Macbeth was a simpleton, this was it.

'You'll never guess what I have tae tell you, sir,' said Blair. 'Macbeth has brought the local seer, Angus Macdonald in. Someone left this local weirdo a bottle o' whisky on his doorstep and he's about to drink some of it when he sees his dead mither calling to him from the other side and decides it's poisoned.' Blair laughed and laughed. The voice on the other end of the phone squawked and the laughter died on Blair's lips. Mr Daviot was a Lowland Scot in love with the Highlands and everything Highland. Seers were Highland and therefore to be treated with respect. 'Well, if you say so, sir,' mumbled Blair and put the phone down.

'I've to take this whisky tae Strathbane fur analysis,' he growled, 'and you and Macdonald here are tae go along to the hotel and see the super. They'll be naethin' in that bottle but straight Scotch, and then you'll look like the fools you are.'

Mr Daviot treated Angus with great courtesy, ushering him tenderly to an armchair and handing him a cup of coffee.

Angus told his story to an appreciative audience this time. 'And I gather that Macbeth here went to see you to ask what Mrs Thomas had wanted to know,' said Mr Daviot. 'Did you tell him?'

'I was about to,' said Angus, 'when I got that fright. Och, she didn't want to know anything. She offered me a fiver for thae wally dugs on my mantel, but I ken they're worth a bit these days. I told her greed would be the end of her.'

'And why did you say that?' asked Mr Daviot sharply.

'I hae the second sight,' said the seer.

'You may just have had it today,' said Hamish. 'But it's my guess you'd heard about Trixie already and you were cross because she was trying to cheat you out of your china dogs. I'd better take you back, and look about and we'd better get forensic up to your cottage.'

'You gang along yourself,' whined the seer. 'I've a mind tae stay here wi' Mr Daviot. He has the sign of greatness in his face.'

That was enough for Mr Daviot so Hamish left with only Towser for company.

The wind had dried the ground and he was doubtful whether the forensic team would be able to find a footprint. The path to the back door was formed of paving stones and outside the back gate was springy heather moorland.

If someone had tried to poison Angus then that someone must have known Hamish was going to call on him. But according to Blair, the whole village knew of Hamish's proposed visit. He strolled over the moorland at the back of the cottage and found himself looking down on Iain Gunn's farm. He wondered whether either Blair or his detectives had interviewed Gunn. He had not told Blair about the bats, having felt it to be of not much importance. Now with the cloud shadows chasing each other across the moorland and with the soughing of the wind, Iain Gunn seemed like someone who ought to be taken seriously. All he would have had to do was to run up the hill to the back of the seer's cottage and leave that whisky. Hamish suddenly remembered the look of hate on Iain's face as he watched Trixie leaving. He would need to tell Blair and Blair would rightly point out that he had been withholding valuable information.

Iain Gunn was in his farmhouse kitchen, just removing his Wellington boots, when Hamish arrived. His son, a tall, gangling youth, was sitting at the kitchen table and Mrs Gunn was stirring something in a pot on the stove.

'It's yourself, Hamish,' said Iain cheerfully. 'Sit down.'

'I would like a wee word with you in private,' said Hamish.

Iain and his wife exchanged an odd look and then he said slowly. 'Come ben.'

Hamish followed him through to the living room. It was bleak and cold and had a little-used look despite the new, fitted carpet on the floor, the plastic flowers in vases, the noisily patterned nylon curtains at the window, and the three-piece suite of acid green uncut moquette.

There was a large television set in one corner but Hamish was sure the Gunn family hardly ever had time to look at it. They all worked hard.

'What's the trouble?' asked Iain.

'Trixie Thomas's death's the trouble. I have to interview everyone who might have had a grudge against her. Now Angus Macdonald is swearing blind someone left a poisoned bottle of whisky outside his back door today.'

'Angus drinks so much it's no wonder that whisky tastes like poison to him now,' said Iain. 'And what could I have had to do with that silly bitch's death?'

'With her out of the way, you could go ahead and bulldoze that ruin,' pointed out Hamish.

Iain gave a derisive laugh. 'That damn fool bird society she started has no doubt written letters to every other bird society, telling them about the bats. I'll have bird watchers trekking over my land and making a pest of themselves. Do you mind the days, Hamish, when bird watchers were nice kindly people you were glad to see? Oh, a lot of them are still fine, but there's a new breed o'militants. The men have got beards and wear camouflage jackets and those wee half-moon glasses and they've got bad teeth and the women have got their fat bums stuffed into jeans and wear anoraks covered with badges. I'd shoot the lot of them if I thought I could get away with it. No, I didn't poison Mrs Thomas, Hamish.' He leaned forward. 'Look, just think of all the hassle a man has to put up with from the government these days. Look how Scotland has changed with value added tax hit squads and petty little bureaucrats enjoying throwing their muscle around. There's a lot more folk I had better reason to kill than Trixie Thomas. You'll probably find her man bumped her off. It's aye the husband.'

'Why?'

'Imagine living with a woman who irons creases in her jeans and wears white sneakers.'

'Aye, it's enough to turn the strongest stomach,' said Hamish with a grin. Then his face grew serious. 'Look, Iain, I didnae tell Blair about the bats and I'll need tae tell him, so prepare yourself for a hassle.'

'Don't worry. I had the income-tax inspector round last week. If I can put up with an income-tax inspector, I can put up with Blair.'

Hamish made his way back up past Angus's cottage and met the seer coming up the hill.

'They are not interested in my story any mair,' said Angus peevishly. 'They haff arrested the husband.'

'Paul Thomas? Why?'

'No' him. Her first husband.'

'Her –?'

'Aye, it turns out that lodger o' theirs, John Parker, used tae be married to her.'

Hamish went straight to the hotel. John Parker was closeted with Blair and his two detectives in the hotel room allocated to the police. Hamish put his head round the door.

'Get lost,' snarled Blair.

Hamish walked away. He wondered where Daviot was. As the local policeman, he, Hamish Macbeth, should have been in on the interrogation.

He saw the hotel manager in the forecourt. 'Where's Mr Daviot?' asked Hamish.

'He's gone back to Strathbane. There's been a successful drug raid on one o' the ships,' said Mr Johnson. 'This murder's become small beer.'

Hamish made his way to The Laurels. Paul Thomas was working in the garden.

'What's all this about her first husband?' demanded Hamish.

Paul straightened up from his weeding slowly and passed an earthy hand over his forehead. 'It was a surprise to me,' he said in a bewildered way. 'Why didn't Trixie tell me?'

'Did you hear them having a row or anything?'

'No, they went on like strangers. It was probably him that did it. And I don't care anymore. Nothing's going to bring her back.' Tears rolled down his cheeks and Hamish patted him awkwardly on the shoulder.

'Can I have a look at his room?'

'It's full of forensic people, dusting everything in sight although they've already dusted everything and I don't know what they hope to find. I wish everyone would go away and leave me alone.'

Hamish went back to the police station in time to meet Priscilla who was just driving up.

Although he was glad to see her, he found with surprise that his heart no longer gave a lurch. They sat in the kitchen and Hamish told her about the seer and the first husband.

'You would think it would be one of the locals trying to poison Angus,' said Priscilla after listening in attentive silence.

'Why?'

'Well, someone was very afraid that Angus might have divined something, and only the locals would think that. I can't see either Paul Thomas or this first husband believing in the second sight.'

Hamish poured more tea. 'I think that a frightened murderer might be prepared to believe anything. I hope he doesn't go ahead

114

and arrest John Parker without any evidence. I would like to have a word with him.'

'Blair's capable of anything. Oh, that's clever,' said Priscilla, noticing the screen door.

'It was a couple of American tourists gave me the idea,' said Hamish. 'I wish I could have a word with that Carl Steinberger. He was staying there at the Thomases for a couple of nights. Where was he from again? I know, Greenwich, Connecticut. He may be back home now. Excuse me a minute, Priscilla. I'll phone the police in Greenwich and ask them if they know Carl Steinberger's phone number.'

He was halfway out of the kitchen when Priscilla rose to her feet. 'Don't worry, Hamish,' she said. 'I think I'll call on Angela Brodie. I'm worried about her.'

Hamish stopped. 'Why?'

'She makes me uneasy. You can't go around taking on someone else's personality without something cracking,' said Priscilla.

She drove down to the doctor's house, thinking about Hamish Macbeth. Although he had been as friendly as ever, something had gone out of that friendship. Hamish was no longer shy of her, she thought, nor was his whole mind on her when she was there. She felt uneasily that part of his mind had dismissed her.

Priscilla walked up the path to the kitchen door and then stood motionless, with her hand on the doorknob. From inside came a faint humming sound, a familiar sound. A picture of Trixie rose vividly in Priscilla's mind. She pushed open the door and went in.

Angela was sitting spinning wool, her thin face intent. She was wearing jeans and sneakers and a shapeless white T-shirt with the legend Save The Bats emblazoned on the front.

She looked up and saw Priscilla. 'Oh, Miss Halburton-Smythe,' said Angela, getting to her feet. 'Would you like a cup of coffee?'

Priscilla looked around the gleaming and sterile kitchen. Angela put beans – from Nicaragua, where else? thought Priscilla – into the coffee grinder. Priscilla sat down at the kitchen table. It was amazing, reflected Priscilla, how a hairstyle could alter a woman. Angela's perm showed no signs of growing out. Hard little curls rioted over her head, making her hair look like one of those cheap wigs from Woolworths. Her mouth appeared to have become thinner with little tight lines at the corner of the mouth.

'I didn't know you had a spinning wheel,' said Priscilla.

'Paul gave it to me,' said Angela. 'Poor man. He didn't want to keep it in the house. He said every time he looked at it, he could see Trixie sitting there.'

'How are things going?' asked Priscilla.

'Not very well,' said Angela, feeding coffee into the machine. 'The meeting of the Anti-

Smoking League was last night. And do you know how many turned up? Two. And one of them was that layabout, Jimmy Fraser, who thought it was a stop smoking class.'

'That might be a better idea,' said Priscilla. 'You might get more results by helping people to stop smoking than by putting a sort of prohibition ban on the stuff.'

'Anyone in their right mind should know it's dangerous to smoke.'

'But it's an addiction, like drinking, like eating too much sugar. I read an article which said that addicts are more open to suggestion as to how to stop than outright militant bans. Look at Prohibition in the States with people drinking disgusting things like wood alcohol and going blind. I'm sure a lot of people drank more during Prohibition than they would have done if the stuff was available.'

Angela folded her lips into a stubborn line. 'Trixie used to say that people didn't know what was good for them. They need to be taken in hand.'

'You can make a lot of enemies, Mrs Brodie, if you try to be nanny to the world.'

'That's a bitchy thing to say!'

'And so it was,' said Priscilla contritely. 'I'm concerned for you, Mrs Brodie. You seemed a happier person before Trixie Thomas arrived on the scene.'

'I was half alive,' said Angela fiercely. 'There's so much to be done in the world.

Trixie used to say that if everyone just sat around doing nothing, then nothing would be done.' She took a deep breath and said triumphantly. 'I am declaring Lochdubh to be a nuclear-free zone.'

'Oh, Mrs Brodie! You yourself?'

'I'm forming a committee.'

Priscilla felt at a loss. There was something badly wrong with Angela Brodie. She wondered whether the doctor's wife was at the menopause. She had grown even thinner, not the willowy slimness she had had before, but a brittle thinness. Her fingers were like twigs and there were deep hollows in her cheeks. Priscilla suddenly wanted to get out. An old-fashioned fly paper was hanging from the kitchen light and dying flies buzzed miserably, trapped on its sticky coating.

'I've suddenly remembered something,' lied Priscilla, getting to her feet. She could not wait any longer in this suffocating atmosphere for that coffee to fill the pot, drip by slow drip.

She turned in the doorway. 'Do you know, Mrs Brodie, that Angus Macdonald claims someone tried to poison him today by leaving a bottle of poisoned whisky outside his door?'

'Silly old man,' snapped Angela 'It's years since he did a day's work. Him and his silly predictions.'

Priscilla went outside and took a deep breath of warm damp air. The wind had dropped and a thin drizzle was falling. She wondered how Hamish was getting on with his phone call.

Hamish had found everything remarkably easy. The police in Greenwich, Connecticut, knew Carl Steinberger. He owned a small electronics factory outside the town. They gave Hamish the number and Hamish dialled and asked for Carl Steinberger.

In his usual Highland way, Hamish did not get right to the point but waffled on about the screen door and the flies and the weather until Mr Steinberger interrupted him gently with, 'Look, officer, it's great talking to you, but I'm a busy man.'

'Can you tell me what you made of the Thomases?' asked Hamish. 'The wife's been poisoned.'

'Jesus! What with?'

'Arsenic.'

'Rat poison? Something like that?'

'We can't find anything,' said Hamish. 'That other lodger, John Parker, turns out to be her first husband.'

'I can't tell you anything,' said Mr Steinberger, 'except that we didn't like her. My wife said she had a knack of making her husband look like a fool, but we didn't pay much attention. The place was clean and the food was good. She was a great baker. We must have put on pounds. But there was no fun in eating her cakes because her husband was on a diet and he would sit at the table and glare at every crumb of cake we put in our mouths. That John Parker took his meals in his room and typed when he wasn't out walking. Can't tell you any more.'

Hamish thanked him and put down the phone. He wondered what John Parker was saying to the detectives. He went along to the grocery store and bought a bottle of whisky, wondering whether he should go out with his gun that night and bag a few brace of the colonel's grouse to sell in Strathbane and so make up for all the whisky he was having to buy.

He wandered back along to the hotel and stood outside, looking at the fishing boats.

At last, he heard Blair's loud voice. He went to the wall of the hotel. Blair was standing with his back to him facing his two detectives. There was no sign of John Parker. One of the detectives, Jimmy Anderson, looked across to where Hamish's head was appearing above the wall. Hamish raised the bottle of whisky and Anderson gave a brief nod.

Hamish then went back to the police station and settled down to wait.

After half an hour, Anderson appeared. 'If ye want me to tell ye about it,' he said, 'give us a drink first. Blair's fit tae be tied. Can't make a case against Parker.'

Hamish poured the detective a glass of whisky and said, 'So what's Parker's background?'

'Ex-drug addict. Hash and a bit of cocaine. Out of work. Along comes Trixie Thomas. Social worker. Takes him in hand. Sees his writing. Badgers publishers and agents. Gets him started. Gets him off drugs. Gets him earning. And then what do you think she does?'

'She divorces him,' said Hamish.

'How did you know?'

'I don't know,' said Hamish slowly. 'Just a lucky guess. Anyway, is he still in love with her? Did Paul Thomas know he was her ex? He must have known when he married her. Told me he didn't, but surely he did.'

'No, he says Trixie reverted to her maiden name after the divorce.'

'Still, he must have known. She'd need to have her divorce papers, surely.'

Anderson grinned. 'Seems the managing Trixie arranged everything and all he can remember is standing in the registrar's office saying yes.'

'And when did all this take place?'

'This year.'

'And when did she divorce Parker?'

'Ten years ago.'

'Any children?'

'No, she couldn't have any. What about some more whisky?'

Hamish poured him another glass. 'So how did Parker know where to find her?' he asked.

'She wrote to him. She'd heard about him selling the film rights. Must have been in some magazine. She said she needed boarders and he owed her something because she never had asked him for alimony, and she didn't want Paul to know, but it would be a nice way of paying her back for the start she had given him in life and all that crap. So the wimp comes up. He was paying her two hundred pounds a week. Paul didn't know. She collected the money ... cash. No income tax, no VAT.'

'Leave a will?' asked Hamish.

'Aye, left everything to Paul. He owns the house already but she left twenty thousand pounds.'

'Not bad for someone who was aye pleading poverty,' said Hamish. 'But not enough to kill for. Look, maybe you can help me out of a jam.' He told Anderson about Iain Gunn and the bats.

'I'll tell Blair,' said Anderson. 'He's so hell bent on proving Parker did it, he'll hardly listen.'

'Look,' said Hamish urgently. 'I'm going along to have a word with Parker. If the results of that bottle of whisky come through, let me know.'

'Okay,' said Anderson, draining his glass. 'Keep the bottle handy.'

John Parker was typing in his room when Hamish called.

'Now, Mr Parker,' said Hamish severely, 'what I want to know is why you told an outright lie when you said that you hadn't known Trixie Thomas before?'

'I've got a lot of work to do,' said John. 'I didn't murder her and I didn't want to be the subject of a police inquiry. You've probably heard I used to be on drugs and I've been on the wrong side of the law several times in the past. I have no great liking for policemen.'

'And I have no great liking for liars,' said Hamish coldly.

'Sorry about that, copper, but that's the way it is.'

'So tell me about your marriage.'

'There's nothing much to tell. I was a right mess when Trixie found me. She got me into a drug clinic, paid for it herself, found my manuscripts when I was in there, and when I came out, she took me around agents and publishers. She corrected my manuscripts and typed them. She did everything but go to the toilet for me,' he said with sudden savagery. 'Look, it's hard when you have to be perpetually grateful to someone. When she said she was divorcing me, I could hardly believe my luck.'

Hamish raised his eyebrows. 'Then why did you come back?'

He sighed, a little thin sigh. 'I suppose I still felt grateful to her – really grateful. I wanted to see her again.'

'And when you saw her?'

'It was all right.' His voice held a note of amazement. 'She not only had Paul, she had the village women in her control. The lodgings were comfortable and the place is pretty. I've got a lot of work done.'

Hamish looked at the typewriter. The author was beginning chapter ten of a book, witness to the fact he spoke the truth. 'Luke Mulligan,' Hamish read, 'smiled down at Lola who was holding on to his stirrup and an odd look of tenderness flitted across his craggy features.'

Beside him on the desk lay a pile of manuscript with the title page on the top. It read, 'The Amazon Women of Zar'.

Hamish pointed to it. 'Doesn't sound like a Western.'

John Parker's grey, neat features took on an even more closed look. 'It's science fiction,' he said curtly. He rose and picked up the manuscript and opened a battered suitcase and popped it inside. All at once Hamish longed to see what it was about.

'What were the relations between Mr and Mrs Thomas?' he asked.

'Fair enough,' said John. 'Regular marriage. She fussed over him like a mother hen, but he seemed to like it.'

Hamish stood up. 'I suppose you have been told not to leave the village.'

'Yes. That man, Blair, is determined to accuse me of the murder. In fact, he would have done so if I hadn't threatened to sue him for wrongful arrest.' Hamish stood up to leave. His eyes roamed around the room. Whatever antique furniture Trixie had managed to get from the locals, she must have taken it all down to the auction rooms. John's room furnishings were white and modern, the sort of units bought in Inverness and assembled at home.

'I believe from the village gossip that you're a friend of the Halburton-Smythes,' said John Parker.

Hamish looked surprised. 'I am by way of being a friend of the daughter,' he said. 'Colonel Halburton-Smythe does not have much time for me. Why do you ask?'

'I would like a look around the castle.'

'It's not very old,' said Hamish. 'It's one of those Gothic monstrosities built in Victorian times.'

'Nonetheless, I might be able to use it in a book.'

Hamish thought quickly. If he could be sure John Parker was up at the castle, then he might be able to get a look at that manuscript he had been so anxious to hide.

'I think I could fix that for you,' said Hamish. 'What about tomorrow?'

'Suits me.'

'I'll phone Miss Halburton-Smythe and then come back and tell you what she says.'

Hamish went back to the police station just as the detective, Jimmy Anderson, was arriving.

'Let's have another drink,' pleaded Anderson. 'Blair's fuming and shouting. It was arsenic, all right, in that old fortune-teller's bottle.'

'That'll bring the press in droves,' said Hamish gloomily. 'Good story. I Saw My Own Death, Says Seer. So what's Blair up to?'

'He's threatening to arrest Angus Macdonald tomorrow.'

'Why?'

'Impeding the polis. He says the auld gnaff put the stuff in the whisky hisself so as to get the press to write about him.'

'Could be.'

'Now Daviot's breathing fire and vengeance. Says if Blair doesn't wrap up the case fast, he'll put someone else on it.'

Hamish shook his head sadly. 'It's a daft thing to say to a man like Blair. He'll now arrest the first person he thinks of.'

'Well, let's have that drink.'

They sat talking about the case until Anderson realized that Blair would be anxious to get back to Strathbane and would be looking for him.

After he had left, Hamish phoned Tommel Castle and asked to speak to Priscilla.

'Miss Halburton-Smythe is not at home,' said Jenkins.

'Look, get her to the phone, you horrible snob, and do it fast or I'll come up there and knock your teeth in,' said Hamish pleasantly.

When Priscilla answered the phone, she said, 'What did you say to Jenkins? He was cringing and creeping and saying he didn't know I was in the castle and yet he'd just served me a drink before you called.'

'Never mind. I want you to do something for me.' Hamish told her about John Parker and asked her to keep him at the castle for an hour at least.

'Oh, very well,' said Priscilla. 'What about having dinner with me at the hotel tomorrow night?'

'I don't know if I'll manage to be free by that time,' said Hamish. 'I feel I'm getting on to something on this case.'

There was a short silence and then Priscilla said, 'All right. Another time, maybe.'

Hamish thanked her and put the phone down. Priscilla stood by the phone, looking thoughtfully at the receiver before she replaced it. Hamish Macbeth would never have turned down an invitation to dinner before. Perhaps he had a girlfriend. Priscilla suddenly felt very bad-tempered indeed and went off to give the butler a lecture about lying to friends who tried to get her on the telephone.

Hamish picked up his cap, called to Towser, and went out on his rounds. It was Friday night and he would need to go to the pub to make sure no one was thinking of drinking and driving.

As he was passing the Maclean's cottage, he heard angry voices and then a woman screamed loudly. He ran to their door, opened it, and walked in.

Archie and his wife were standing on either side of the kitchen table. She was holding her cheek as if she had just been struck.

'What's going on here?' demanded Hamish.

'You interferin' bastard,' howled Archie. He came round the table towards Hamish with his fists raised. Towser crept under the kitchen table and lay down. Hamish stretched out a long arm and seized Archie by the wrist and then deftly twisted his arm up his back. 'Tell me what's going on, Archie, or I'll break your arm.'

'Leave my man alone,' screeched Mrs Maclean. 'We were having a wee bit row, that's all.' Hamish's quick eye noticed she was standing, holding something behind her back, and he was sure that if she had not been so determined to conceal that something then she would have leapt to her husband's defence.

'Aye, leave us be,' growled Archie.

Hamish released him and shoved him into a kitchen chair. He took out his notebook and pencil. 'Begin at the beginning,' he ordered. 'What happened?'

'Whit are you taking notes fur?' raged Archie. 'I'll have you fur this, Macbeth. Have you a search warrant? Whit right have you to walk into a man's home?'

One minute it seemed to the Macleans as if Hamish was standing at his ease, looking down at his notebook; the next, he had moved like a flash around the back of Mrs Maclean and wrested what she was holding from her hand. She shouted something and tried to claw his face, but he jumped back. Under the table Towser whimpered dismally.

Hamish looked at the can in his hand. Dead-O Rat Poison.

'Well, now,' he said quietly, looking at their stricken faces. 'Well, now.'

'It's naethin's to dae with this,' said Mrs Maclean. 'We hae the rats. I got that frae the grocers the other day.'

'You realize I shall question Mr Patel and find out exactly when you bought it,' said Hamish.

There was a long silence. 'She didnae get it from him,' said Archie at last. 'I got it myself from Iain Gunn over at Coyle.' He rounded on his wife. 'If you had kept your mouth shut . . .'

'Me!' she said furiously. 'Then whit was it doing at the back o' your drawer o' underpants?' She put her hands up to her mouth and stared at Hamish with frightened eyes.

'Well, Archie?' asked Hamish, and when he did not reply. 'It's tell me or come with me to Strathbane and tell Blair.'

'I'll tell ye,' said Archie wearily. He looked at his wife. 'I found it at the back o' the kitchen cupboard, hidden in that old tin marked FLOUR. I took it tae ma room for safekeeping.'

'You silly wee man,' said his wife. 'Did you no' remember our Jean and the weans were coming for tea? Wee Rory's only two year,' she explained to Hamish, 'and he's aye under the kitchen sink, taking out things. I hid it so the child wouldnae find it. I've had it for a year. We had rats in the shed in the garden.' Hamish ran over in his mind what he knew of the Maclean family. Jean was their daughter and she had three small children, the ferreting two-year-old, Rory, being one of them.

'So,' said Hamish, 'you thought, Archie, that your wife might have poisoned Mrs Thomas, and you, Mrs Maclean, thought your husband might have done it. My, my. Trixie Thomas must have caused some rare rows. I'll need to take this. Where did you get it?'

'I got it from Patel a year ago,' mumbled Mrs Maclean. 'Ye cannae blame me. Holding hands wi' that wumman. He never held hands wi' me, not even when we was courting.' She put out a red hand towards Hamish with an oddly pathetic, pleading movement. It was almost deformed with years of being immersed in boiling water, bleach and ammonia. Her wedding ring was embedded in the swollen flesh below the red shiny knuckles.

'I'll need to report this to Blair the morrow,' said Hamish sadly. 'I'll take this can with me.'

As Hamish looked at the couple, he thought viciously that had Trixie Thomas still been alive, he might have murdered her himself. The Macleans' marriage, which had plodded along for years quite happily, would never be the same again.

He whistled to Towser and walked outside. It was a clear night, the rain had lifted, and great stars burned in the heavens. Towser slunk behind his master. 'You,' said Hamish looking down at the animal, 'are a coward.' Towser licked Hamish's hand and slowly wagged his tail. 'But you're a decent dog and I'd rather have you a coward than savaging the sheep,' said Hamish. He stooped and scratched the dog behind the ears and Towser leapt up and down in an ecstacy of joy at being forgiven.

The Patels' shop was in darkness, but Hamish went around the side and mounted the stairs that led to the flat over the shop. After some time, Mrs Patel, wearing a bright red sari, answered the door.

'Och, Mr Macbeth,' she said impatiently, 'whit d'ye want at this time o'night?'

It always surprised Hamish to hear a Scottish accent emitting from such exotic features. He said he wanted to speak to her husband and Mrs Patel reluctantly let him in. Their living room was bright and gaudy with a three-piece plush suite in bright red, still covered with the plastic casing it had been delivered in. A huge display of plastic tulips in a woven gilt basket sat on a carved table top, which was supported by four carved elephants. Everything smelled strongly of curry. Mr Patel came in. He was a small brown man with liquid brown eyes and a beak of a nose.

'Evening, Mr Macbeth,' he said. 'Will ye be havin' a wee dram?'

'Not tonight. Mr Patel, you were asked if you had sold any rat poison and you said you hadn't and yet Mrs Maclean told me she had bought some here a year ago. It's called Dead-O.'

'I thought you meant recently! Aye, I got about two dozen frae a wholesaler in Strathbane a year ago. Used it myself. No' very good. Didnae even slow them up.'

'You realize what this means?' said Hamish gloomily. 'Blair will want me to go around every house in the village tomorrow collecting cans of rat poison.'

'Keep ye out o' trouble,' said Mr Patel with a grin. 'Why bother yer heid about Blair anyways? That man's a pillock.'

'A pillock who is senior to me in rank. Now, Mr Patel, I don't suppose you can remember who bought it?'

'I can remember Mrs Wellington had a can for the mice in the church. I hadn't any mouse poison and she didn't want traps so she said she'd try the rat stuff. Then there was Mrs Brodie, the doctor's wife. Mice, too.'

'Anyone else?'

'Let me see. Oh, I ken. The estate agent for the Willets, them that used to own the Thomases' place. It had been standing empty for so long that they were getting rats in, or so they thought.'

Hamish thanked him and then phoned and left a message for Blair about the rat poison. Then he went to see John Parker, who told him that Miss Halburton-Smythe had phoned and had invited him up to the castle at ten in the morning. Hamish knew Blair would have him searching for all those other cans of poison, but that would give him a good excuse to read that manuscript John Parker had been so anxious to hide.

He said good night and then made his way back along the waterfront to the pub. An ordinary common or garden Scottish Highland drunk would come as a relief.

Chapter Six

I am silent in the club
I am silent in the pub,
I am silent on a bally peak in Darien;
For I stuff away for life
Shoving peas in with a knife,
Because I am at heart a Vegetarian.

No more the milk of cows
Shall pollute my private house
Than the milk of the wild mares of the
  Barbarian;
I will stick to port and sherry,
For they are so very, very,
So very, very, very Vegetarian.
                        – G.K. Chesterton

It was the detective, Jimmy Anderson, who arrived at the police station first thing in the morning with the expected orders from Blair to search the village for rat poison. 'Anything left in that bottle?' he said hopefully.

'At eight o'clock in the morning!' exclaimed Hamish. 'Come back later. Is Blair all ready to meet the press?'

'He's blinding and blasting but he's got his Sunday suit on and his hair's all slicked down aboot his horrible ears,' said Anderson with a grin.

Hamish shut Towser out in the garden and set off. Mrs Wellington, the minister's wife, was his first call. She was in her kitchen. Her husband was poking distastefully at a bowl of muesli with his spoon. 'Sit down,' ordered Mrs Wellington when she saw Hamish, 'and I'll give you a cup of coffee.'

Hamish sat down at the kitchen table. 'That's a good, healthy breakfast,' said Hamish to the minister. Mr Wellington put down his spoon with a sigh. 'I cannot think starvation is good for anyone,' he said. 'I feel like a child again – if you don't eat it, you won't get anything else.'

'Well, that's the way to the Kingdom of Heaven,' said Hamish cheerfully. 'You know, become like a little child again.'

'Don't quote the scriptures to me, Macbeth,' said the minister testily. 'Why are you here?'

Mrs Wellington put a mug of coffee in front of Hamish. He took a sip and coughed. 'I am here to look for a rat poison called Dead-O. What is this coffee, Mrs Wellington?'

'It's dandelion coffee. Mrs Thomas showed me how to make it.'

Hamish sadly pushed his mug away.

'You see what I mean?' said the minister. 'Why not stay for lunch? We're having nettle soup.'

Hamish ignored him. 'The rat poison,' he said. 'You bought some from Patel about a year ago. You had the mice.'

'So we did,' called Mrs Wellington over one large tweed shoulder. She was scrubbing dishes in the sink with ferocious energy. 'Not very good. I think the mice just left of their own accord.'

'Have you any of the stuff left?' asked Hamish patiently.

'No, I threw it out months ago.'

'You are sure?'

Mrs Wellington turned around and put her soapy hands on her hips. 'I am not in the habit of lying, Mr Macbeth.'

'I'd better go and try somewhere else,' said Hamish, getting to his feet.

'Oh, but you haven't had your coffee,' said the minister sweetly.

'It's all rush.' Hamish picked up his hat and headed for the kitchen door. The minister followed him outside. 'When is it all going to end?' he asked mournfully. 'I dream of large T-bone steaks and mounds of fried potatoes. You know, Mr Macbeth, I think all that wretched Thomas woman did was give the women of Lochdubh an opportunity to persecute their husbands. There's a strong bullying streak in women, lying down in there, always waiting to be tapped.'

'Perhaps when the murder is solved, they'll all go back to normal,' said Hamish. 'When's the funeral?'

'It's today, at three this afternoon.'

'It surprises me to know Mrs Thomas was a member of the Church of Scotland.'

'She wasn't,' said the minister. 'She wasn't a member of anything. But her husband wants her to have a Christian burial.'

'Are any of her family from England going to be present?'

'No. That's the odd thing. Her parents are dead and she had no sisters or brothers, but usually someone has some sort of aunt or uncle or friend who would like to come along. Perhaps she was unpopular.'

'Yes,' said Hamish slowly. 'I think if she had lived, she would have gradually become very unpopular here. Mind you, someone hated her enough to murder her. Did she get any furniture from you, any ornaments?'

'Yes,' said Mr Wellington, growing angry. 'We had a Victorian ewer and basin that belonged to my grandparents. My wife gave her that. I was furious. Those things are valuable these days.'

Hamish stood for a moment, looking across the rain-pocked loch. 'While I'm searching for rat poison,' he said, 'I may as well try to find out if she got her hands on anything really valuable.'

'An as yet unrecognized Rembrandt?' said the minister. 'It was amazing what she got out of people when you consider that the dealers are always calling around those old croft houses and village houses in the hope of a bargain. Why, old Mrs MacGowan on the other side had been plagued by dealers for years but she's too crafty to let anything go. Mrs Thomas was going to call on her. I wonder whether she was successful or not?'

Hamish had not called on Mrs MacGowan for some time. She was a lonely, crusty old woman and he did not enjoy visiting her, but felt it his duty to call in on her from time to time and make sure she was well. She could easily drop dead one of these days, he reflected, and no one would know.

'I'd better be on my way,' Hamish said, taking out a stick of repellent and wiping his face with it, 'before the midges make a meal of me. Blair will be in a bad temper. The attempted murder of Angus Macdonald is bound to bring the press in hordes.'

'I wouldn't be too sure of that,' said the minister. 'Angus was interviewed by television and several newspapers before the last election for his prediction. He got it all wrong and since then no one outside Lochdubh has shown any interest in him. Do you think he really saw something?'

'Yes,' said Hamish. 'For once in his lying life, I think he must have actually had some sort of forewarning.'

He made several more calls in his search for rat poison and then at ten o'clock, he made his way to The Laurels. Paul was chopping logs. He was fatter, his stomach hanging over his trouser belt as he bent to his work. When Hamish said he was going to take a look at John Parker's room but did not want the writer to know, Paul answered with an indifferent shrug and went on with his work.

Hamish climbed the uncarpeted staircase to John Parker's room. In Victorian times when the villa had been built the stairs would have been thickly carpeted and the rooms over-furnished. There was a bleak air about it now, a smell of pine and disinfectant and wood smoke and cheap soap, rather like a youth hostel.

John Parker's room was not locked. Hamish opened the door and went inside. There was no sign of that suitcase but he found it eventually on top of the wardrobe and lifted it down. He opened it and took out the pile of manuscript. He sat down on the bed and started to skim quickly through 'The Amazon Women of Zar'.

Hamish reflected he had read some silly stories in the past, but this took the biscuit. The men were the slaves of the women and there were several colourful purple passages about how the men were called in each night of the full moons – Zar had five moons – and made to have sex with the women. He yawned and read on. Then the hero, Luke Jensen, who, like the Luke Mulligan of the Western, also had a craggy face, got hold of the rare and forbidden plant, Xytha, which was guarded by a three-headed monster, Zilka, and brewed a poison from it which killed the leader of the Amazon women, whereupon her bossy acolytes turned into nubile blonde bimbos, cooing over the men, and thanking Luke for having turned them back into 'real women' again.

Hamish put down the manuscript. Had Trixie been John's Amazon woman? The leader of the women bore a startling resemblance to Trixie although she wore a brass brassière and chain and leather loincloth instead of un-bleached linen smock, blue jeans and sneakers.

He carefully returned the manuscript to the suitcase and the suitcase to the top of the wardrobe and went downstairs. Mrs Kennedy was in the kitchen with her pallid children.

'I thought you would have been allowed home by now,' said Hamish.

'Aye, we're going in a couple o' days,' said Mrs Kennedy. 'I decided tae stay on. I'm no' payin' rent and the fresh air's good for the bairns.'

'I'm sure you've told the CID this already,' said Hamish. 'But what brought you here? I know Mrs Thomas advertised in the *Glasgow Herald*.'

'I phoned up the Sutherland tourist board,' said Mrs Kennedy, 'and they telt me this new place wus cheap.'

'What does your husband do, Mrs Kennedy?'

'I hivnae got one,' she said cheerfully.

'Then, what does the father of your children do?'

'Which father?' she said with a coarse laugh. 'I cannae remember them all.'

'You shouldn't say such things in front o' the children,' said Hamish furiously.

'Ach, take yersel' off, ye damp soda scone,' jeered Mrs Kennedy.

And Hamish did that, cursing himself for having wasted his time trying to appeal to the finer feelings of what was surely a Glaswegian prostitute. Despite the regeneration of that city, Glasgow still had some of the ugliest prostitutes in the world, and Mrs Kennedy probably shoved her bulk into a corset on Saturday nights and her swollen feet into high heels and trawled the pubs looking for someone blind drunk enough to buy her services.

He decided to drive up to Tommel Castle and get the key to Mrs Haggerty's cottage and try to find out if Trixie had found anything valuable. It was only when he drove up and parked in the front of the castle that he realized with amazement and with a sharp sense of loss that his mind was totally on the case and he was not hoping for a meeting with Priscilla.

But Colonel Halburton-Smythe did not know that. He said with obvious relish that Priscilla was out in the grounds somewhere with Mr Parker, and handed over the cottage key.

Hamish hesitated. 'I would like to ask you again – what was your opinion of Mrs Thomas?' he asked.

'I've already told your superior officers all I know,' snapped the colonel and turned away.

Hamish went out and drove over to Mrs Haggerty's cottage. It had an abandoned, lost air about it. He unlocked the door and went in. There was an old-fashioned kitchen with a box bed in a recess, a small dark hall, a living room crammed with furniture and knickknacks and photographs, and a toilet. No bathroom. Although he knew very little about antiques, Hamish was sure there was nothing of value left in the crowded living room. There were sepia photographs on the walls and on the tables of men with walrus moustaches and women in enormous hats. Mrs Haggerty had died at the age of ninety-eight and had not left a surviving relative behind, or any that anyone knew of. Still, the colonel should not have allowed Trixie to take anything until it became absolutely sure that no one was left to inherit the bits and pieces. And there were many of those. Mrs Haggerty had obviously found it hard to throw anything away. There were cupboards full of old Christmas cards and magazines and recipes and jam jars and bottles.

There was even a bundle of fly papers, brown and smooth to the touch. He wondered whether their stickiness had vanished with age.

He heard a sound outside and then the door of the living room opened and Priscilla walked in. She looked cool and neat in a white silk blouse and tweed skirt, sheer tights, and polished brogues. As usual, her bright hair fell in a smooth curve to her shoulders and the calm oval of her face was luminous in the gloom of the cottage parlour.

'Thank goodness Parker has left,' she said. 'Gave me the creeps. Oily little man.'

Hamish looked at her with interest. 'I thought he was quite ordinary and pleasant. What's up with him?'

'Oh, he's perfectly polite, but too polite, if you know what I mean. Kept thanking me and thanking me and saying what a lot of trouble he must be putting me to until I felt like smacking him, like a fly, splat!'

'You should read about the strong silent men in his books,' said Hamish, 'with their whipcord muscles and their craggy faces softening with tenderness.'

'Inside every weak man there's a macho man who only gets out on paper?' said

Priscilla with a laugh. 'I know a woman in London who writes romances and hasn't got one romantic thought in her mind off paper. Oh, look at this old photograph. What splendid hats the women wore then.'

Did Priscilla ever have any romantic thoughts, Hamish wondered, studying her as she bent her head over the framed photograph she had picked up. And yet, she had had an inner glow when John Burlington had been around.

'Heard from that Burlington fellow?' he asked.

'Mmm? Oh, yes, he writes and phones regularly. He seems to be making tons of money.'

'And you like that?'

'I admire successful people, and talking about success, how's the case going, Sherlock?'

'I'm still groping about in the dark,' said Hamish mournfully.

'Suspects,' said Priscilla briskly. 'There's the husband, Paul. All that shattering grief could be an act.'

'Aye, and then there's Parker. Sneaky and weak enough to use poison. Who else?'

'Well, there's poor Dr Brodie. He's been drinking a lot recently. Looks miserable. Says he feels his wife has been taken over by a creature from another planet.'

'Archie Maclean or Mrs Maclean,' said Hamish. 'Trixie Thomas ruined that marriage.'

'And there's Iain Gunn.'

'What, over a lot o' wee bats?'

'The bats are no more. You should have servants, Hamish. An endless source of useful gossip. It fell down last night, Gunn says.'

'Then he probably did it himself and I'll hae the devil of a job proving it,' said Hamish. 'But he wouldn't kill just to get a wee bit more land.'

'Oh, yes he would. Or rather, that's the gossip. He craves land and more land. You know what land greed's like.'

'Fair enough, but I thought all that talk about Gunn's greed was jist caused by jealousy. May-be they could be right. Either there's someone else we haven't thought of or that's the lot o' suspects.'

'Has Mrs Kennedy's background been gone into?'

'It would have been and if there had been anything there, Anderson would have told me.'

'Well, there's Angus Macdonald.'

'Why him?'

'Look at it this way.' Priscilla leaned forward eagerly and he caught a whiff of French perfume. 'He lost face over that wrong prediction about the general election. He could have poisoned that whisky himself.'

'And killed Trixie Thomas first? Come on, Priscilla.'

'I suppose it is rather far-fetched. But he could still have poisoned that whisky. I mean,

Hamish, you don't believe in the second sight, do you?'

'Yes, I do. I think there's a handful of people who get a brief insight about something that's going to happen about once in their lives. It's hard to prove. So many people say after a disaster or a death that they had a premonition.'

'Where are you off to now?' asked Priscilla in surprise as Hamish made for the door.

'I'm off to continue to look for cans of rat poison called Dead-O. Could you ask the housekeeper if she ever bought any? Here's the key for the cottage.'

He raised his hand in farewell and walked out. Priscilla crossed to the window and watched him go. She felt a little sad that Hamish did not seem to show the old eagerness to be in her company.

Hamish drove into the village and parked outside the Brodies' house.

Angela was in the kitchen, sitting at the table, reading something. He brightened, thinking she had returned to her old ways until he saw she was reading a recipe for vegetarian lasagne.

'I came to ask you if you bought some rat poison called Dead-O about a year ago,' said Hamish.

'No, we've never had rats. Wait a bit. We had mice and I bought some rat poison.'

'Have you still got it?'

'Come out to the shed and we'll have a look.'

He followed her into the garden. The shed was scrubbed and clean. All the cans of pesticide on the shelf above the door were gleaming, and forks and hoes and spades were all polished as well.

'I'm proud of this,' said Angela. 'I gave it a good clean out only the other day.'

Hamish took out a handkerchief and gently lifted down a can of Dead-O. He twisted open the top. It was half full.

'You used a lot,' he said.

'I hate mice. Nasty things. Of course, I was so slapdash then, I never read the instructions, just put down saucers of the stuff all over the place. It certainly got rid of the mice. Now, is there anything else? I'm very busy.'

'You'll be going to the funeral,' said Hamish.

'Yes, of . . . of course.'

Hamish touched his cap. 'I'll see you there.'

Everyone had turned out for Trixie Thomas's funeral, even Mrs Kennedy and her brood. The church was noisy with the sound of women weeping as Mr Wellington read the service and grew louder as the congregation followed the coffin to the graveside in the churchyard on the hill above the church.

Paul Thomas was being supported by two of the men from the village and looked on the point of collapse. Dr Brodie was standing beside Hamish. 'I'd better give that man a sedative and put him to bed as soon as this is over,' he said.

'I'd look to your wife as well,' said Hamish. 'She's in a bad way.'

The doctor's face hardened. 'Silly bitch,' he said viciously and Hamish wondered whether he meant Trixie Thomas or his wife.

After the graveside service was over, everyone went to The Laurels where Mrs Wellington was presiding over the funeral baked meats. Whisky was poured out all round and gradually the atmosphere began to lighten. One man told a joke, another capped it, and soon the gathering began to sound like a party.

The men of the village were glad that Trixie Thomas had been laid to rest.

Hamish saw Iain Gunn and went over to join him. 'I'm surprised to see you here,' said Hamish.

'I never miss a funeral,' said Iain, taking another glass of whisky from a selection of full glasses on a table.

'I hear that old building of yours mysteriously fell down,' said Hamish.

'Aye, providential that. I'll hae no more trouble from the bird people.'

'But you'll have trouble from me,' said Hamish. 'I have to investigate that building and make sure you didn't do anything to it to make it collapse.'

'Wouldn't ye be better off finding the murderer than harassing a poor farmer over some flying rats?' sneered Iain. 'But you'll find nothing, I can assure ye o' that.'

'Did a good job on it, did you?' said Hamish cynically.

Blair came rolling up, a glass in one meaty hand. 'Listen, copper,' he snarled, 'hae ye got all these cans o' rat poison yet?'

'No, I'm still looking.'

'In the bottom o' a glass? Hop to it, sonny.'

Iain Gunn sniggered as Hamish left.

Hamish walked around The Laurels and went in the door at the back. The small Kennedy child called Susie was eating a huge lump of cake.

'Bad for your teeth,' said Hamish.

'Get lost,' said the child, her voice muffled by the cake. He made for the door and she said, 'or give me some money for sweeties.'

'No,' said Hamish. 'Not a penny will you get. Didn't Mrs Thomas put you all on a vegetarian diet?'

'Naw, only her man. She couldnae risk scaring off her lodgers wi' that rubbishy stuff, my maw says. Went on and on aboot sugar bein' bad and stuffing her face wi' cakes the whole time when she thought naebody was looking.' Her sharp face took on an evil, gloating look. 'Want tae know what she and her man got up to in the bedroom?'

'No, I do not,' said Hamish roundly and made his way through the door from the kitchen that led into the main body of the house. He edged back into the sitting room where the funeral reception was being held in time to see Blair taking his leave. He waited a moment and then edged his way into the room and called loudly for silence. They all turned to face him. Priscilla was there, he noticed. Of course, she would be. It was expected of her. She was wearing a black dress and a small black hat.

'I am looking for cans of a stuff called Dead-O,' said Hamish. 'Patel was selling it a year ago. It's a rat poison. If you have any, bring it along to the police station as soon as you can.'

Mrs Wellington bustled up, looking outraged. 'How dare you make such an announcement at a funeral?' she demanded. 'It's mercy poor Mr Thomas has gone to lie down.'

'I have to find those cans of poison,' said Hamish patiently. 'Pretty much the whole of Lochdubh is in here. It saves me going all around the houses.'

By evening, he was satisfied with the result. He had fifteen cans of rat poison in front of him. Not a bad haul out of the two dozen that had been sold a year ago. The cans were all neatly labelled by Hamish with the name of the person who had bought it.

* * *

Dr Brodie stood in the doorway of the kitchen and surveyed first his wife and then his dinner. Salad with goat cheese. He had told her and told her he could not eat such food and she had told him that she was not going to poison him by serving him with greasy steaks and chips any more. She was as hard as flint.

He felt he was not addressing Angela but some strange creature who had invaded his home.

'I want a divorce,' he said.

Angela looked startled. 'Don't be silly. Don't you realize I am doing all this for you? The healthy food, the clean house, no wine or spirits?'

'You're doing it because you are a nasty little bully like your friend, Trixie. I'm glad someone poisoned her. I hope she had a bad time dying. I've phoned Pollet, the lawyer, in Strathbane already and told him to draw up the divorce papers.'

Angela's face was as white as paper. 'On what grounds?' she demanded.

'Breakdown of marriage. Oh, well, thank goodness the hotel's gone back to old-fashioned cooking. Good night, *dear*.'

Dr Brodie walked along to the hotel. He did not feel anything much at all. His wife had died some time ago, as far as he was concerned, and he was merely getting divorced from the domestic monster who had taken her place. There was something lightening about the idea that that Trixie woman was six feet under. 'Pushing up organic daisies,' he said, and began to laugh.

'What's the joke?' asked Police Constable Hamish Macbeth. He, too, was heading towards the hotel, carrying a box of eggs under his arm.

'Come and celebrate,' said the doctor. 'I've just phoned Strathbane and arranged for the divorce papers to be drawn up.'

Chapter Seven

The common cormorant or shag
Lays eggs inside a paper bag
The reason you will see no doubt
It is to keep the lightning out.
But what these unobservant birds
Have never noticed is that herds
Of wandering bears may come with buns
And steal the bags to hold the crumbs.

                                         – Anon.

'Look,' said Hamish awkwardly, 'I know you haff had the hard time, but couldn't you wait a bit?'

'No,' said the doctor, 'I've made up my mind.'

'Aren't you being a bit hard on Mrs Brodie? Have you ever considered she might be suffering from the menopause? Women go a bit odd then.'

Dr Brodie snorted. 'That's all a lot of cobblers. It's all in the mind. Women have been told they go odd at the menopause and use it as an excuse.'

'Well, you're the doctor, but there's been an awful lot about it in the newspapers lately,' said Hamish. 'And there's been an awful lot about lazy National Health doctors who don't keep up wi' the latest research. I know Mrs Thomas was an awful woman, but the trouble with her was a lot of the things she said were right. You know smoking's bad for people and high cholesterol food's bad for people . . .'

'I've never had a day's illness in my life,' snapped the doctor. 'It was being treated like a child that I couldn't bear. Eat your greens, pah! No sudden rush into vegetarianism. Coax the child with smaller and smaller portions of meat and larger and larger bowls of salad, until it's only salad with the occasional nut cutlet thrown in for comic relief. She even served me dandelion coffee but I took the lot and threw it in the loch. Don't interfere in my life. I've made up my mind and that's that.'

The television screen above the bar flickered into life. Angus Macdonald's face beamed down on them. He began to tell a highly embroidered account of his vision.

'I didn't think they'd bother with Angus, considering he got the election results wrong,' said Hamish.

'Too good a story,' said Dr Brodie. 'They were all up at the hotel today and then they went on up to Angus's cottage. He'll be drunk for a month.'

Angus's image faded, to be replaced by the strong features of Mrs Wellington. 'Mrs Thomas was the perfect wife,' said Mrs Wellington. 'She brought new life into the village. No one here wished her ill. It must have been some maniac from outside.'

'Join me for dinner,' offered Dr Brodie, draining his glass.

Hamish shook his head. 'Why don't you take your wife? You used to do that. Wouldn't it be a good idea to sit down and discuss this divorce like a couple of grown-ups?'

Dr Brodie sighed. 'Maybe you're right. I'll see.'

Hamish looked around the bar. Bert Hook, the crofter, was getting very drunk. Hamish went over and removed his car keys and told him to collect them at the police station in the morning.

He went outside and walked along the waterfront, wishing with all his heart that the murderer could be found and that the village could return to its normal quiet. He loved his peaceful, uneventful life in a way that Priscilla, say, could never understand. In fact, this was not the age when anyone could understand an unambitious man. The night was calm and still and a full moon floated through the clouds.

'Hamish?'

Hamish stopped and looked down at the man in front of him. Hamish had been so engrossed in his thoughts that he had not seen him approaching. He was small and dapper, wearing a good tweed jacket and flannels, collar and tie. He had neat, clever features and thin hair.

'Good evening,' said Hamish cautiously.

'Don't you recognize me?'

Hamish slowly shook his head.

'It's me. Harry. Harry Drummond!'

'Neffer!' Hamish turned Harry round so that the light on the harbour wall fell full on his face. 'Harry Drummond,' he marvelled.

For Harry had been the village drunk before he left to go to Inverness to get treatment. He had been a swollen, hairy bundle of evil-smelling rags when Hamish had seen him last.

'You've changed beyond recognition,' said Hamish. 'Are you back here again?'

'No. I've got a good job as a bricklayer in Inverness.'

'You'll be taking the wife down there to live with you, then?'

'No, Hamish. The fact is, she wants a divorce.'

Hamish stared at him in amazement. Phyllis Drummond's devotion to her drunken husband had been the talk of the village. She stood by him through thick and thin, taking on cleaning jobs to keep food on the table, suffering the occasional beating with never a word of complaint.

'But why?' asked Hamish. 'Is the whole of Lochdubh going in for divorce? Man, she should be delighted with you the way you are now, and you with a good job and all.'

'No, she ups and says she cannae stand me, that I was better when I was on the drink. Women! I've been up here trying to get her to change her mind but she willnae listen.'

They both turned as Dr Brodie came running up. 'She's gone,' he panted. 'Angela's gone.'

'Mrs Brodie's probably up at the church hall at one of her meetings,' said Hamish soothingly.

'No, I'm telling you, she's gone. She's smashed up the kitchen and she's gone.'

'I'll phone for reinforcements and then I'll look for her,' said Hamish. 'Harry, go round and get all the men in the village.'

He ran back to the police station and phoned Strathbane. Then he got in his Land Rover with Towser beside him and drove off. Clouds had covered the moon and the night was pitch black. Where on earth should he begin to look for her? In the loch? On the moors? In the sea?

He searched all night, unwilling to give up although reinforcements had arrived from Strathbane and policemen were combing the lochside and policemen and villagers were

fanned out over the moors and a police helicopter hummed overhead.

The next morning was sunny although the
air was still heavy and damp and the sunlight
had that threatening, glaring look which her-
alded bad weather to come.

He finally stopped the Land Rover and
stared bleakly through the windscreen. If
Angela Brodie were suicidal, then where
would she go? Or if she were merely badly
distressed, where would she go to put a dis-
tance between herself and her husband? He
looked up at the twisting, soaring peaks of the
Two Sisters, the giant mountains above
Lochdubh. He left Towser fast asleep in the car
and began to climb.

Bees droned in the heather and heather flies
danced in the sleepy air. Up he went through
the heather and bracken. He took off his jersey
and laid it down on a rock and put his cap on
top of it. He rolled up the sleeves of his blue
shirt and set off again. Once, when he had
been very upset by Priscilla – how long ago
and far away that seemed now! – he had
climbed high above the village to a ledge of
rock to sit and be alone with his misery. It was
a chance, a slim chance, that Angela Brodie
might have chosen the same route. The ground
rose steeply and he sweated in the warm air.
Midges stung his face as his sweat washed the
repellent from it. For an hour he toiled
upwards towards where he remembered the

ledge to be. His disappointment was sharp when he at last reached it and found no one there. He sat down, unshaven and exhausted. Below him he could see the small figures of the searching police on the moors and then, as he watched, a van drove up to the harbour and frogmen got out. He was so very tired. His head swam and he longed to lie down and sleep. But somewhere in all the miles of mountain and moor and loch was Angela Brodie.

And then his eyes sharpened. A tiny figure was struggling down far below the ledge. He leapt to his feet and tumbled down from the ledge and began to run. His feet went from under him and he slithered down, grabbing at heather roots to break his fall. At last he stopped and stood up, panting, and looked wildly around. There was the figure still below him and staggering on from side to side like a drunk.

His long legs bore him towards that fleeing figure until with a feeling of pure gladness he saw that it was Angela Brodie. A final burst of speed brought him up to her and he flung himself on her and brought her down on to the heather.

He sat up and turned her over. Her face was swollen with crying.

'Come along,' he said gently. 'You're in a bad way.'

'Can't go back,' she said drearily.

'We all have to go back to it sometime,' he said. 'Come along. I've got a flask of brandy in the Rover.'

He helped her to her feet. She made an effort to pull herself away and then collapsed in a heap at his feet. He picked her up in his arms and carried her down towards where the Land Rover was parked. He laid her down in the shade of it and got the flask of brandy from the glove compartment and forced it between her lips. She spluttered and her eyes opened.

'That's better,' said Hamish. 'Now, you'll soon be home.'

'I don't w-want to go home,' she said. Tears spilled down her cheeks. He took out a hand-kerchief and wiped them away.

He gathered her in his arms and stroked her hair. 'There, there,' he said. 'Tell Hamish all about it.'

'John wants a divorce.'

'That's what he says, but men often say things in a temper they don't mean.'

'He meant it. John never says anything he doesn't mean.'

'Maybe not before. But you gave the man every reason to lose his temper. He wasnae divorcing you, but Trixie. He wasnae living with you, but Trixie. You even tried to look like the woman.'

She shivered despite the heat. 'I feel so lost and empty,' she wailed.

'That's maybe a good sign. You feel a bit

empty when an obsession's left ye,' said Hamish, thinking of Priscilla.

'You see, Trixie seemed to have all the answers,' said Angela mournfully. 'I've felt so useless for years. I go down to Glasgow or Edinburgh or even Inverness and people say, what do you do, and I say, I'm a housewife, and they say, is that *all*? Trixie said that housewifery was a noble art and if it were done properly then it could be very satisfying. I got a high from all the work and all the committees. It was like being drunk. She praised me and no one had done that in ages. She told me John was killing himself with his cigarettes and cheap wine and greasy meals. I l-love John.'

'He seemed awfy happy with you the way you were,' said Hamish, still gently stroking her hair. 'Come on back wi' me.'

She twisted away from him. 'I can't.'

He looked at her thoughtfully. There was more up with Angela Brodie than the sudden loss of her adopted personality.

'You think your husband killed Trixie,' he said flatly.

She went very still.

'Look, I felt like killing her myself,' said Hamish. 'But I didn't do it.'

'"Yet each man kills the thing he loves,"' quoted Angela drearily.

He looked at her oddly. 'You're really in a bad way. Home and bed for you.'

'But there's a meeting of the bird society

163

tonight. Lord Glenbader, the Duke of Anstey's son, is bringing over some specimens from the castle collection!'

'I'll see to it myself.'

Hamish rose and snapped his fingers and Towser leapt into the back. He helped Angela into the Land Rover. He ran back up the hillside and collected his jersey and cap. Clouds were covering the sky and the wind had a chill edge to it now. He took a flare gun out of the back of the Land Rover and fired it into the sky and watched for a moment while one green star hung against the tumbling back clouds to tell the searchers below that Angela Brodie had been found.

Mrs Wellington and two of the village women arrived at Dr Brodie's and silently began to clean up the shattered mess of the kitchen, sweeping up shards of crockery and glass, wiping up the mess of flour and coffee grounds and broken jars of jam from the floor.

Hamish helped them, putting the broken glass and china into cartons, taping it up and driving it off to the council tip. When he returned, Mrs Wellington was taking mugs out of a box and hanging them up on the hooks. 'Poor Mrs Brodie didn't leave anything to drink out of,' she said, 'and I had these put by for the church sale. Put on the kettle, Mr Macbeth, and we'll have a cup of tea.'

'Is it just the kitchen she wrecked?' asked Hamish. He opened a cupboard and took out a can of cat food and two cans of dog food to feed the family pets.

'No, come and look in the living room.'

Hamish put down the can opener and followed her into the other room. The mirror above the fireplace had been smashed.

'Couldnae stand the sight of herself,' he said mournfully.

'Havers,' said the minister's wife, who had no time for psychology, 'she was probably drunk.'

They returned to the kitchen. Hamish fed the spaniels and the cat and put the kettle on. Dr Brodie came downstairs from the bedroom. 'How is she?' asked Hamish.

'Sleeping,' he said wearily. 'Will this misery never end?'

'Be very kind to her when she wakes,' said Hamish anxiously. 'If she's still in a bad way, you might consider taking her down to Strathbane for some therapy or something like that.'

'I don't believe in all that rubbish. If everyone just pulled themselves together and got on with life, there would be no time for crackpot psychiatrists.'

'For a village doctor, you're a walking disaster,' said Hamish crossly. 'I am glad I am never ill. What would you prescribe? Eye of newt?'

'Leave the doctor alone,' ordered Mrs Wellington. 'Have you no feelings?'

Hamish went out and left them to it. He headed for the police station, dying for sleep. Then he saw the press standing outside it, interviewing Blair.

He swore under his breath and drove straight past. Blair saw him and shouted something but Hamish was too tired to care. He drove up to Tommel Castle. As he swung in at the gates, he saw one of the gamekeepers and stopped and rolled down the window. 'Colonel at home?' he asked.

'No,' said the gamekeeper. 'Himself and the wife has gone to Inverness.'

'Good,' said Hamish and drove on to the castle entrance.

Jenkins would dearly have loved to tell him that Priscilla was not at home but the young lady had given him such a ribbing about lying to Hamish that he did not dare. Priscilla came running down the stairs and stopped short at the sight of Hamish. 'You look awful,' she said. 'What's happened to you?'

'It's Angela Brodie,' said Hamish, stifling a yawn. 'She's cracked. But she's back home in bed now.'

'Oh, you found her. I heard she had gone missing. How is she?'

'Physically, she's all right. I hope her mind's in better shape when she wakes up. I need sleep, Priscilla, and Blair's at the police station. Can you spare me a bed for an hour?'

'Yes, I'll take you up to one of the guest rooms. Where's Towser?'

'In the car.'

'Wait here. I'll fetch him.'

Soon Towser came lolloping in at her heels. She led master and dog up the shadowy staircase and into a guest room and turned down the blankets. 'There's a bathroom through there, Hamish, and you'll find disposable razors in the cabinet. There are clean towels and everything. John was hoping to fly up. He's got his own helicopter now. But he couldn't make it. Put your shirt and underwear outside the door and I'll have them washed for you. When do you want up?'

'Give me two hours,' said Hamish. 'Oh, Priscilla, there's that damn bird society tonight. I told Mrs Brodie I'd run it for her, Lord Glenbader's coming to give a talk.'

'You amaze me, Hamish. He doesn't preserve birds except under aspic.'

'I know, he's a pill. But I have a feeling there won't be much of an audience. People are losing interest in all these societies and committees. Could you round up a few people?'

'Certainly. I'll get on the phone right away. Now, go to bed.'

She went out and closed the door. Hamish removed his clothes and put his underwear and shirt outside the door and then climbed into bed. Towser leapt on the bed and stretched out across his feet. 'Get down,' ordered Hamish sleepily. Towser rolled his eyes and stayed where he was.

Two hours later, Priscilla came in carrying his clean clothes over her arm. Constable Hamish Macbeth was lying fast asleep, his ridiculously long eyelashes fanned out over his thin cheeks. Towser opened one eye and lazily wagged his tail.

The bedclothes were down around Hamish's waist. It was amazing how muscular Hamish was, thought Priscilla, looking at his naked chest and arms. His red hair flamed against the whiteness of the pillowcases and he looked young and vulnerable in sleep.

He opened his hazel eyes suddenly and looked straight at her. A look of pure happiness shone in his eyes and then it slowly died, like a light being turned down.

'Two hours up already,' groaned Hamish. 'I could have slept all day.'

'Here are your clothes,' said Priscilla briskly, 'and I've got some people to go to the bird meeting. Come downstairs when you're ready and we'll have tea.'

It was a black day in the life of Jenkins, the butler. To have to serve Hamish Macbeth tea in the drawing room hurt his very soul.

When Hamish returned to the police station it was to find the detective, Jimmy Anderson, waiting for him.

'So you're back,' said Anderson. 'I've been left here to give you a row for sloping off.'

'I see you've made yourself at home,' said Hamish. Anderson was sitting in the police station office with his feet on the desk and a glass of whisky in his hand.

'Aye, thanks. Blair's right sore at ye for finding that Brodie woman. Daviot turned up to see how the search was going on and Blair told the super that it was thanks to his brilliant detective work that Mrs Brodie had been found. He was well launched on his story when my friend and colleague, Detective MacNab, who had been insulted earlier by Blair pipes up and says, "Oh, but it was Macbeth what found her. Brought her down from the hill himself. We was all looking in the wrong direction." Blair looks fit to kill. The super accuses him of trying to take credit away from you, and Blair says he was simply describing how the operation had worked, and that he had sent you up the mountain himself. "That cannae be true," says MacNab, "Weren't you just saying you hadn't seen Macbeth?" You should hae seen Blair's face. I couldnae bear it any longer and walked away, but it wouldnae surprise me if Blair doesn't get MacNab back walking the beat before a month is up. Blair's gone off to grill Parker again, just for the hell o' it.'

'How did you get on with Halburton-Smythe?' asked Hamish.

Anderson groaned. 'Whit a bad-tempered wee man! How dare you waste my time when you could be out looking for the murderer. That sort o' thing. Asked him what Mrs Thomas had taken from the cottage and he looked sulky and said it was some old china and glass and bits of furniture and odds and ends in a box. She was a sterling woman, according to his nibs. She certainly seemed to have a way with her. Was she all that attractive?'

'Not strictly speaking,' said Hamish. 'But she had a very forceful personality. Type of person you love or loathe.'

'Well, I'd better be toddling along,' said Anderson. 'Consider yourself reprimanded. What are ye going to do now?'

'I think I'll jist go along to The Laurels and see how Paul Thomas is getting on,' said Hamish. 'I like that man. I think when he gets over his wife's death, he'll settle down here all right.'

Paul Thomas was sawing up a dead tree at the back of the house.

'Feeling better?' asked Hamish.

'Still a bit shattered,' said Paul. 'But I find work helps. I'll be glad to see the back of that Kennedy woman and her rotten kids. Trixie could cope with that sort of person and pointed out we had to take anyone while we were getting started, but she whines the whole time and the only reason she stayed on was because I couldn't bring myself to charge her rent, because that would have meant shopping for her and cooking for her.'

'How do you get on with Parker, now that you know he's her ex?'

'We've become pretty friendly. In fact, he's been a great help. I want to talk about her, you know, and he's prepared to listen.'

'You know we found Mrs Brodie?'

'Yes, it was all over the village.'

'I'm running that bird society for her tonight. Want to come?'

'No, thanks. I'll stay here and get on with my work. Truth is, I don't know anything about birds.'

He should have come, thought Hamish that evening as Lord Glenbader started his lecture. It would have made two of them. Lord Glenbader obviously didn't know much about birds either. He was also very drunk. The coloured slides of birds had got mixed up with his recent holiday in India, a fact of which he seemed quite unaware since he talked down his nose and with his eyes closed.

'And this,' he said, operating the switch, 'is a great barn owl.' His audience solemnly studied a slide of his lordship on an elephant.

'Wrong slide,' said Hamish.

His lordship raised his heavy eyelids. 'Is it? Dear me. Find the right one, constable. There's a good chap.'

Hamish looked despairingly at the great pile

171

of slides. 'It would take all night to look through these,' he complained.

'Then stop interrupting.' Lord Glenbader's eyelids drooped again. 'And this ish a houshe martin,' he slurred. A smiling Indian beggar appeared, holding out a hand for baksheesh.

Priscilla came in carrying a pot of coffee, poured a cup of it, and handed it to Lord Glenbader. 'Thanks,' he said. 'And here's a lot of tits.' He peered down Priscilla's low-necked blouse and Hamish sniggered. But the slide did show three blue tits and two coal tits. It was hit and miss from then on, Lord Glenbader only occasionally describing the right slide. The audience sat, numb with boredom.

Priscilla steadily poured coffee. Lord Glenbader's lids gradually rose. 'What a bore all this is,' he said crossly after the hundredth slide. 'What I need is a good drink.'

'What are all these plastic bags?' asked Priscilla.

'Oh, them. They're Victorian specimens of stuffed birds from my great grandfather's collection. I'll pass them round. Don't take them out of the bags. Just peer inside. You'll get arsenic poisoning if you handle them.'

'Why arsenic?' asked Hamish sharply.

'That's the way the Victorians kept the bugs at bay,' said Lord Glenbader. 'It was their sort of DDT. The fellow who arranged these things in the glass cases ten years ago got a chesty cough and running at the eyes and jelly limbs.

172

Brodie diagnosed flu. Went to hospital in Strathbane, not believing Brodie and found he'd got arsenic poisoning from handling the birds. Brodie's a fool.'

The Highland audience of men, women and children politely peered inside the bags and then showed the first signs of interest that evening as Priscilla started laying out plates of cakes and biscuits beside an enormous pot of tea. 'Least I could do,' whispered Priscilla to Hamish. 'Rodney Glenbader is a crashing bore.'

Lord Glenbader was now obviously in a very bad mood indeed, made worse by the fact that there was nothing stronger to drink than tea and by the knowledge that he was not being paid for his services. There is nothing more outraged than a British aristocrat who finds he has performed a service for nothing. Lord Glenbader came from a long line of grasping ancestors. He snatched up his birds and stuffed them in a sack and went out, slamming the door behind him.

'Help me with the tea, Hamish,' said Priscilla. 'You're off in a dream. What are you thinking of?'

'I'm thinking of arsenic,' said Hamish. He joined her nonetheless and took the heavy teapot from her hands.

Mr Daviot, the police superintendent came in. 'I'm going back to Strathbane,' he said to Hamish. 'Congratulations on finding Mrs Brodie.'

'I had luck on my side,' said Hamish.

'We could do with a few able men like you on the force in Strathbane,' said Mr Daviot.

Hamish opened his mouth but Priscilla said eagerly, 'You couldn't have a better man, Mr Daviot. He's a genius at solving crime.'

'Well, I wish he would solve this one,' said Mr Daviot. He waved his hand in farewell.

'I wish you wouldn't speak for me, Priscilla,' said Hamish crossly. 'I have no mind to leave Lochdubh.'

'But you *must* have, Hamish. You can't want to remain an ordinary copper for the rest of your life.'

Hamish sighed. 'When will you get it through your head that it's not clod-hopping stupidity or shyness that keeps me here. I love Lochdubh, I like the people, I'm happy. Why should I go and get a rank and money to please society's accepted idea of success? I *am* successful, Priscilla. Very few folk are contented these days.'

'I made a mistake about that Macbeth fellow,' said Mr Daviot as he undressed for bed that night. 'I think he's very bright.'

'Are you sure?' His wife adjusted a hair net over her rollers. 'The colonel and Mrs Halburton-Smythe didn't seem to like him at all.'

'But the daughter does, and I think there might be a marriage in the offing.'

'Oh.' His wife digested this piece of intelligence. 'Wheh don't we esk them for dinner?'

'Wait till this case is solved, if it ever is solved,' said her husband, climbing into bed.

Hamish went to The Laurels after the meeting was over. Paul Thomas answered the door himself. 'Come in,' he said. 'I was watching television.'

Hamish went in to the sitting room. The Kennedy family were lined up in front of the set. In front of them was a coffee table with a plate of sticky cakes. From the electric light above their heads, a fly paper hung, brown and flyless.

From upstairs sounded the busy rattle of John Parker's typewriter.

'What can I do for you?' asked Paul, picking up a cake and stuffing it whole into his mouth. His eyes were fixed on the television screen. *L.A. Law* was showing.

'Wondered if there was anything I could do for you?' said Hamish.

Paul did not reply. He picked up another cake and sat down on a chair beside the Kennedys, his eyes still on the screen.

Hamish decided if the man was that interested in watching television, he must have made a good recovery from his breakdown at the funeral.

No one in the room noticed Hamish leaving.

175

Chapter Eight

Tut! I have done a thousand dreadful things
As willingly as one would kill a fly.
                                    – Shakespeare

Hamish drove over to inspect the ruin on Iain Gunn's farm. Three-quarters of the building had collapsed, leaving one end standing up, the two floors still showing scraps of coloured wallpaper on the cracked plaster.

He puttered among the ruins, shining his torch. If there was any proof that Iain had done the job himself then that proof was buried under the rubble.

And then he heard a faint squeak. He shone his torch up to the rafters of the bit of the house which was still left standing. Small furry bodies hung in rows upside down.

Bats.

He heard the noise of an engine and switched off his torch and walked outside on to the field.

Iain Gunn was approaching in a bulldozer. Hamish felt irritated. Iain had no right to attempt to bulldoze the building until he got the all clear. As he walked forward and held up his hand, he was vividly reminded of that day when the women had mounted their protest. He could still see Trixie, the leader of the women – leader of the Amazons? – her eyes glowing with excitement and hear that cockneyfied voice of hers.

The bulldozer ground to a halt.

'You can't go on with it, Iain,' called Hamish. 'You've still got bats in the bit that's left and anyway, you shouldn't have attempted to knock it down until you got the okay.'

Iain looked at him, a blind, flat look. He started up the bulldozer again.

'Stop!' shouted Hamish, standing in front of it.

The bulldozer moved steadily towards him.

Hamish swore and leapt to one side and as the bulldozer came alongside, he jumped on it and ripped the keys from the ignition.

Iain Gunn punched him on the face and sent him flying.

Hamish scrambled up from the ground and leapt back on the bulldozer and seized the farmer by his jacket and dragged him out so that he fell face down on the ground. He knelt on his back and handcuffed him, deaf to the stream of abuse that was pouring from the farmer's mouth.

'Now, on your feet,' said Hamish grimly.

Iain staggered to his feet and stood, head down. 'Leave me alone, Hamish,' he said wearily. 'I'm sorry I hit you, but don't you understand what a load o' rubbish this all is? Here's a man who needs more land and there's a bloody stupid law that says he can't do it because o' a lot o' flying vermin. It's *my* land and I should be able to do what I like with it. Damn that Thomas woman for an interfering bitch!'

Hamish looked at him. He should arrest the farmer and charge him with assaulting a police officer and all sorts of other fiddles. It meant paperwork. It meant a court case. It might mean Iain going to prison.

'Turn around,' he snapped.

He unlocked the handcuffs and tucked them away and then he took off his cap and threw it on the ground and put up his fists.

'Come on, Iain,' said Hamish. 'We'll settle this ourselves.'

Iain sized up Hamish's thin, gangling form and began to smile. 'Okay, Hamish, but don't blame me if ye get sore hurt.'

But Iain found it was impossible to hit Hamish. The constable weaved and ducked, dancing lightly on his feet, diving under the farmer's guard to land his punches. At last, Hamish said, 'Let's finish this,' and that was the last thing Iain heard for about ten minutes as a massive punch landed full on his jaw.

When he recovered consciousness, Hamish was kneeling beside him on the ground. 'All right?' he asked anxiously.

'Man, ye've got a sore punch,' whispered the farmer.

'Well, now that the law in its way has been enforced,' said Hamish cheerfully, 'can I hae your word that you'll leave the bats alone?'

'Aye, you hae my word.'

Hamish helped him to his feet, gave him a swig of brandy from his flask and helped him back into his bulldozer and stood waiting while the bulldozer churned its way back over the soft ground.

He decided to go and pay a visit on old Mrs MacGowan and see if Trixie had managed to winkle anything valuable out of her. Perhaps it was simple greed which had caused the murder and Trixie had got hold of something worth killing for.

But as he drove into Lochdubh, he saw he was approaching Harry Drummond's house and, in his usual, nosey, Highland way, decided to find out first what on earth had persuaded Mrs Drummond to divorce a sober and working man when she would not divorce the drunk.

Mrs Drummond was at home. She was a soft, shapeless, dyed blonde of a woman with a face covered in a layer of thick make-up and a sour little painted red mouth like a wound. 'Whit's he done?' she asked when she saw

Hamish on the doorstep and he could swear there was a certain amount of hope in her eyes.

'Harry? Nothing,' said Hamish. 'Can I come in a minute?'

She shrugged by way of an answer and led the way through to the living room, removing a tattered pile of women's magazines from a chair so that he could sit down.

Flies buzzed about the room and she seized a can of fly spray and sent a cloud of it up to the ceiling. Hamish sat in a gentle rain of insecticide and asked, 'Why are you going to divorce Harry? He's looking great and he's got a good job.'

She lit a cigarette and took an enormous drag on it. 'I'm in love wi' somebody else,' she said.

'Who?'

'Buckie Graham, him over at Crask.'

'But Buckie Graham's a terrible drunk wi' a nasty temper!' exclaimed Hamish.

'All he needs is someone to look after him,' said Mrs Drummond defiantly. 'We're getting married as soon as the divorce comes through.'

She offered Hamish a cup of tea in a half-hearted way and he refused. He spent several more minutes trying to persuade her of the folly of marrying Buckie, but she only became extremely angry.

'Women!' he thought, as he drove over to Mrs MacGowan's on the other side of the loch.

181

The cottage was tucked away at the edge of the pine forest. Hamish climbed down from the Land Rover and took a deep breath of sweet pine-scented air. He knew that the inside of Mrs MacGowan's cottage was going to smell as horrible as usual.

'So you've finally decided to come and see me,' said the old woman when she opened the door.

She was bent and gnarled and twisted like an old willow tree but her black eyes sparkled with intelligence. Hamish edged his way into her small parlour. It was crammed with furniture and china and photographs, reminding him of Mrs Haggerty's cottage. Dust lay everywhere and the awful smell of Mrs MacGowan pervaded the close atmosphere.

'I'll just open the window,' said Hamish hopefully.

'Leave it be,' she said. 'The flies just come in.'

'You seem to have caught plenty already,' said Hamish, looking up at the fly paper, black with dead flies, which dangled from the ceiling light. 'Where do people get these things from?'

'It was that Mrs Thomas. Herself got Patel, that wee Pakistani . . .'

'He's Indian.'

'Oh, well, what does it matter. She starts on about this ozone layer, whateffer that might be in the name o' creation, and says these sticky ones are better than spray cans and the wee Indian got some from somewhere.'

'I want to ask you about Mrs Thomas. Did she call on you often?'

'Oh, aye, herself came a lot.'

'What for?'

'She said she wass sorry for me and brought me cakes and scones. But I knew what she wass after.'

'That being?' prompted Hamish.

She nodded her head towards a Welsh dresser. 'That.'

'The dresser?'

'That platter wi' the three women and the man on it.'

Hamish went over and examined it. It had a gold edge and a painted scene showing three ladies in eighteenth-century dress surrounding a courtier. The colours were exquisite.

'Offer you any money?' asked Hamish.

'Och, aye,' she cackled with laughter, 'A fiver.'

'I would say it's worth a lot more than that.'

'When I saw her getting that keen on having it and trying no' to look it, I got Andy, the postie, to bring round his Polaroid and take a picture. I sent the picture tae the Art Galleries in Glasgow and they sent me a wee note. It's up on the shelf above it.' Hamish took down the dusty letter and opened it. The museum had pleasure in informing Mrs MacGowan that her platter appeared to be Meissen, around 1745, with a scene painted after Watteau, but they could not be sure until they examined the platter themselves.

Hamish whistled silently. 'And did you tell her?'

'Not me. I jist kept her coming round wi' the cakes and biscuits and hinting I wass ready to give it away to her.'

'You know you could get a lot of money for that?'

'Aye, but I'll leave it to my great grand-daughter in my will. She can sell it if she wants.'

'So she didn't get anything out of you?' asked Hamish.

'Not a thing, although it wasnae for the want o' trying.'

Hamish asked after her health, made her a pot of tea, presented her with a packet of chocolate biscuits, and got up to leave. He looked in distaste at the fly paper with its load of dead flies.

'If you've got another of these things, I'll hang up a fresh one for you,' he said.

'No, I hivnae. I don't like them anyway. I liked the good old-fashioned kind. Herself was going to get me some. Not from Patel. He could only get the sticky ones. The flies did not stick to the old-fashioned ones. They jist smelled it and dropped dead.'

Hamish got out of the cottage with the usual feeling of relief at finding himself back in the fresh air. He drove slowly back to Lochdubh, wondering what to do next. A movement to the side of the road caught his eye. It was almost as if someone had ducked down when they saw the car.

He stopped and jumped down and walked back a bit. A small bottom was sticking out from behind a bush.

'Come out,' ordered Hamish.

The little figure backed out. Susan Kennedy, the evil-eyed child from The Laurels.

'I thought you were going home today,' said Hamish.

'I'm no' going,' said the child. 'I want tae stay here.'

'Well, you can't. You have to go back to school. Come on. I'll give you a lift back. I've got some sweeties in the car.'

'Whit kind?'

'Chocolate fudge.'

'Okay.' She walked back with him and climbed into the passenger seat. Hamish fished in the box of sweets he kept handy for the local children and handed her a small bag.

'I love sweeties,' she said, putting two in her mouth at once. 'Im o is bid assem.'

'What?'

She swallowed and then said clearly. 'I'm no' as bad as them.'

'Who?'

'The Thomases. I tried to tell ye about what they got up to in the bedrooms.'

Hamish eyed her cautiously. 'Is this about sweets?'

'Aye. She wouldnae let him have any, so he

185

bought cakes and hid them in a box under his bed in his ain bedroom. She wud wait till he was oot, then she would sneak in and steal some. She was greedier than him any day. He shouted at me and told me I was pinching them and she gave me a bar o' chocolate to shut up.'

Hamish drove her to where Mrs Kennedy was standing at the bus stop with the rest of her brood and a large canvas suitcase. She did not seem either glad or surprised at the return of her missing child. Hamish drove up to The Laurels, wondering whether Mrs Kennedy had even noticed the child was missing.

Paul was out but he could hear the clatter of the typewriter from upstairs. He made his way up to John Parker's room.

'Where's Paul?' he asked the writer.

'Out, I suppose.'

'Tell me, did Mrs Thomas have a sweet tooth?'

John Parker laughed. 'It was like a drug with her. She was like a binge drinker, you know, who can leave the stuff alone for weeks and then goes out and gets stoned. She tried to stop Paul from eating the stuff, but she was as bad as he was.'

'It's a wonder she didn't get fat.'

'I think she burnt it up in nervous energy.'

A fly buzzed furiously against the window. Hamish stared at it and then to the writer's surprise, he got up and left the room. He went downstairs to the sitting room and gazed up at the fly paper. Then he stood on a chair and lifted it down. Back at the police station he sat down and put a call through to the forensic department at Strathbane. In answer to his question, they said they would find out and call him back.

He sat at his desk and thought and thought, pieces of conversation buzzing around in his head the way that fly had buzzed in John Parker's room.

Trixie had liked cakes. Trixie had had no time for John Parker after he had come off drugs and got on his feet. Mrs Drummond wanted a divorce from Harry now that he was sober. Lord Glenbader saying arsenic was the Victorian's DDT. Trixie holding hands with Archie Maclean. Dr Brodie singing about killing Trixie. Angela Brodie quoting Oscar Wilde up on the mountain. John Parker and, 'The Amazon Women of Zar'. Mrs MacGowan saying Trixie had promised to bring the good old-fashioned kind. The flies just smelled it and dropped dead. Dead ... dead ... dead. And so his thoughts went on and on.

Would the phone never ring? It was quiet, except for the howl of the Sutherland wind that had sprung up out of nowhere.

Then the phone rang, loud and harsh.

He jumped nervously and picked it up. He listened intently and then slowly put it down. His face was pale and set. He should tell Blair.

But this was one arrest he was going to make by himself.

He walked to The Laurels and mounted the stairs towards the sound of that chattering typewriter. He opened the door.

'Where's Paul Thomas?' he asked.

'Went rushing off,' said the writer. 'I said you'd been around asking about his Trixie's sweet tooth, and he rushes off like a bat out of hell.'

Hamish ran out of the room and down the stairs. John Parker shrugged and began to type again.

Hamish ran towards the police station, stopping everyone he could on the way, asking for news of Paul. He had been seen heading out through the village and last seen going along the long promontory which divided the loch from the sea.

There was no road along the promontory. Hamish started to run harder. The wind screamed and tore at his clothes. He ran round the side of the hotel and out along the promontory. Jimmy Anderson stood at the hotel window and watched him go. He turned around. 'Something's up,' he said to Blair who was slouched in an armchair watching television. 'Macbeth's just gone running past.'

'Probably the water bailiff's after him,' said Blair, keeping his eyes on the screen.

The promontory ended on the Atlantic side in a small cliff. Silhouetted above the tumbling clouds and right at the edge of the cliff, Hamish saw Paul Thomas. He slowed his frantic pace and walked slowly up to the man and stood beside him. Down below, waves as high as houses, cold and green and stained with the black of sea wrack, crashed on to the rocks below.

'Don't do it,' said Hamish quietly. 'She wasnae worth it.'

Paul sat down suddenly and Hamish sat down beside him on the springy turf.

'How did you know?' he asked.

'I think this is what happened,' said Hamish. 'You were getting on your feet and controlling your overeating with Trixie's help. You came up here to start a new life. You liked doing things, painting the house and working in the garden. But Trixie did not like you doing things and showing any independence whateffer and so she undermined you by taking over and doing them better. You began to eat cakes on the quiet again and she knew that and at last you found out she knew where you hid them and thieved a few for herself. But you loved her, so something bad must have happened. It didn't need to be a man. Maybe she wasn't all that interested in sex. A woman would do for interest. She had Angela Brodie to take over and the rest of the women. She didn't need you any longer. Perhaps she might have guessed that when the novelty wore off, people would like you and not her.

'So she asked for a divorce.'

Paul Thomas remained silent. A huge wave rolled in, the wind whipping the white spray back from the top of it.

Hamish's voice was low and clear and Paul could hear every word despite the tumult of the wind and water.

'You knew if you said you had a toothache and were frightened of the dentist then she would make you go. You had probably been nursing a bad tooth on the quiet for weeks. Before you left, you put the cakes in the box under the bed. But before you did that, you took some of the old fly papers Trixie had brought back from Mrs Haggerty's cottage. I saw that one hanging up in your sitting room and wondered why it wasn't sticky. It was impregnated with arsenic. Trixie told you that. You soaked them in a jug of water and then evaporated the water and got enough arsenic crystals to kill her. Maybe you had read of that Victorian poisoning case where someone did the same thing. Forensic at Strathbane told me about it. I began to remember all sorts of things about the use of arsenic in the last century. It was believed that Napoleon died because of the arsenic in the wallpaper paste in his bedroom. Arsenic was also used widely to keep down bugs. Trixie found that bundle of fly papers. An ordinary person would have found them smooth and decided they were no use and thrown them away. But not Trixie.

190

There had to be a use for everything. She was acquisitive. And so she found out that the old fly papers were covered in arsenic, told you, put the papers away maybe intending to take them over to old Mrs MacGowan some time, and probably forgot about them for the time being. But you didn't.

'You put arsenic in the cakes under the bed, or perhaps just one cake, to make sure. It's a wonder that Kennedy girl didn't eat it by mistake. And so you murdered her.'

'And now I'm going to kill myself,' said Paul, wiping his eyes with his sleeves. 'I hated her so much for wanting rid of me. The house was in her name. She wasn't going to let me have a thing. I was so fat and down and miserable before she came along. No one had ever cared for me so much, not even my own mother. She married me and kept me on a diet. I would have done anything for her. We were going to be so happy here. I laughed about her flirting with Archie Maclean, but I knew she had done it to spite me. She was finished with me and she was out to destroy me. But when she died, I was left with the same mess. Myself. I can't go on living, Hamish. Life hurts, people hurt, I'll just kill myself with food.'

'Now, now, man, isn't prison just the answer?' said Hamish bracingly. 'Think o' it, man. Locked away from cakes. Good exercise, lots of reading, no cruel world to cope with. Better than a health farm any day.'

Can I really be saying all this, wondered Hamish wildly.

'I don't deserve to live,' said Paul.

'Maybe not. But prison will be a hard enough life to make you feel you're atoning for your sins. Discipline. Told what to do from morning to night. What on earth possessed you to try to poison auld Macdonald? You're not a Highlander. You didn't believe he could guess the murderer?'

'I thought she might have told him about the divorce. She didn't want to tell anyone in the village because she wanted to appear the perfect wife until the last minute before the divorce. I heard he was going about saying he could solve the case. I panicked.'

'You're a bad man, Paul,' said Hamish severely. 'Prison's just the place for you. You'll be looked after.'

'Will you come and see me?' Paul sounded like a lost child.

'Aye, I might at that. Come along, man, and get it over with. Now, I'll jist put these nice handcuffs on you to make it all official.' And talking to the big man as if he were a child, Hamish led him back along the promontory out of the sound of the sea.

Mr Daviot, the police superintendent, had made another surprise call on Blair. He was demanding a rundown on the progress of the

Thomas poisoning when Anderson, from his post at the window, turned around with a grin on his face and said, 'Here's Macbeth, bringing in his man.'

'Caught a poacher?' said Blair, getting to his feet, while inside he prayed, 'Look God, please do not let it turn out that Macbeth has found the murderer. Jist dae that for me and I'll never swear again.'

Detectives MacNab and Anderson, Blair and Daviot all crowded at the window, watching as Hamish led Paul Thomas down towards the hotel. The constable was talking the whole time and Paul Thomas had tears running down his face. Hamish stopped and took out a handkerchief and wiped the man's tears away and got him to blow his nose.

'Quick!' said Mr Daviot. 'Downstairs. It looks as if the husband did it after all.'

Hamish had reached the forecourt of the hotel when they came running out.

He looked at Mr Daviot, not at Blair. 'I have charged Paul Thomas with the murder of his wife, Alexandra Thomas.'

'Has he confessed?' asked Mr Daviot.

'Yes,' said Hamish.

Blair heaved a sigh of relief. It didn't take much brains to solve a murder when the murderer just walked up and said he'd done it.

'I'll just take the suspect off tae Strathbane,' said Blair pompously.

'Wait a minute,' said Mr Daviot. 'Come inside, Hamish, and tell us what happened.'

Hamish, thought Blair furiously. The super called him Hamish!

They all walked in to the manager's office and explained to Mr Johnson that they would be using it for a bit. When they were all seated, Hamish told Mr Daviot how the murder had taken place and why.

When he had finished, Blair ground his teeth. The super was looking at Hamish with admiration. Mr Daviot then turned to the big man who was slouched in his chair. 'Do you understand what is going on, Mr Thomas? You know you are being charged with your wife's murder?'

'Yes,' said Paul wearily. 'I wanted to kill myself but Hamish said I would be better off in prison. He said no one could hurt me in prison. I wouldn't have to think for myself.'

Blair opened his mouth to say something and Mr Daviot flashed him a warning look. 'Yes, yes,' said Mr Daviot soothingly. 'Hamish is quite right. Now, we'll just take a statement. See to it, Anderson.'

Mr Daviot took Hamish aside while Paul was drearily confessing to the murder. 'Brilliant work, Hamish,' he said. 'My wife and I would be honoured if you would join us for dinner tonight. We'll drive over here. Eight o'clock, say? And do ask Priscilla to join us.'

Blair moved away. He was shocked and

furious. Like a horrible dream arose the vision of Hamish Macbeth as his superior.

At last, Hamish stood outside the hotel and watched them all drive away. He watched the car bearing Anderson, Blair, MacNab, Daviot, and Paul climbing up the long hill out of Lochdubh until it dwindled to the size of a toy.

Then he strolled back to the police station to phone Priscilla Halburton-Smythe and tell her about the end of the case and that invitation to dinner.

Blair sat in the corner of the dining room at the Lochdubh Hotel that evening. He was no longer furious. He was too miserable for that. His was a dark corner, but he knew the super had seen him, for Daviot had nodded curtly in his direction before turning back to his guests. It wasn't fair, thought Blair, who had turned up in the hope of being included in the party.

Priscilla Halburton-Smythe was wearing a flame-coloured chiffon dress that clung to her figure. Beside her, looking like the lord of the manor, thought Blair enviously, sat Hamish Macbeth, resplendent in a tuxedo which Blair assumed Priscilla had lent him, not knowing Hamish had bought it from a second-hand clothes shop in Inverness that year.

Then Blair noticed that the festive air about the party seemed to be dying fast. He wondered what was up.

Mr Daviot had discussed with his wife Hamish's transfer to Strathbane while they were driving over to Lochdubh. 'Poor chap,' said Mr Daviot. 'He must have hated being tucked away in that backwater. He'll be delighted.'

At first, when he told Hamish the plans for his future over dinner, he did not notice that Hamish was beginning to look more miserable by the minute. 'It means more money and promotion, of course,' said Mr Daviot happily. 'The accommodation is comfortable enough for single men. You won't be able to have your dog there, but I'm sure we'll find him a place in the police kennels.'

'Well,' giggled Mrs Daviot, 'Ay'm sure Hamish won't be single for long.' She gave Priscilla a coy nudge in the ribs with her elbow.

Priscilla laughed. 'Hamish and I are just good friends.'

'Can I have a word in private with ye, Mr Daviot?' said Hamish, deciding it would be better to start addressing the super in a more formal manner.

Mr Daviot looked surprised. Then he looked at his wife who was winking at him and pointing to Priscilla. The superintendent's face cleared. Hamish obviously wanted to talk about marriage plans.

They walked through to the lounge. 'Look, Mr Daviot,' said Hamish urgently, 'you need a policeman here and I am perfectly happy with the job. I do not want promotion. I do not want to work in the town.'

'Why, in heaven's name?'

'I have my home here and my sheep and hens and geese. I have my friends and neighbours. I am a very happy man.'

Mr Daviot looked up at him curiously. 'Are you really happy?'

'As much as a man can be.'

The superintendent felt a pang of pure envy. 'Well, if that's the way you want it. What does Priscilla think about settling down in the village police station?'

'Priscilla is not marrying me. We're just friends. As a matter of fact, she's got a fellow in London.'

Priscilla herself was saying very much the same thing to Mrs Daviot. She was feeling uncomfortable under Mrs Daviot's prying questions and had answered them coldly and then haughtily. Both looked up in relief as the men rejoined them.

Mrs Daviot then saw Detective Chief Inspector Blair for the first time. She was smarting after Priscilla's cold behaviour. Blair was such a nice man, thought Mrs Daviot, meaning that he could be guaranteed to grovel. 'Dehrling,' she said to her husband, 'there's thet naice Mr Blair. Do esk him over to join us for coffee.'

Blair came over, almost at a run. Mr Daviot felt himself begin to relax. There was something so reassuring about Blair. Typical detective. Hamish was odd, eccentric and upsetting. No one really likes to come across a happy and contented man. Besides, as he was not going to marry Priscilla Halburton-Smythe, there was no longer any need to think of him as a social equal.

After dinner, Priscilla and Hamish walked together along the waterfront. She had a long white silk stole about her shoulders and the fringed ends fluttered in the breeze. The wind had dropped and the stars shone brightly overhead.

'So you refused promotion,' said Priscilla flatly. 'What is to become of you, Hamish?'

'Nothing I hope,' he said lazily. 'Obsession's a funny thing,' he said, half to himself, thinking about Angela Brodie, Paul Thomas, . . . and himself. It was so peaceful to be able to stroll along beside Priscilla without being in the grip of that old, terrible yearning.

'People who want to get on in life are not obsessed,' said Priscilla crossly.

'Like John Burlington?'

'Yes, like him. What would the world be like if everyone were like Hamish Macbeth?'

'I don't know,' said Hamish mildly, 'and I don't care either. I don't go about lecturing people on the folly of pursuing a career. That would be silly. Ambition's a grand thing. I wonder what it's like? Still hear from John Burlington?'

'Yes, I'm going back in two weeks' time and he's going to meet me at the airport.'

'And will you marry him?'

'I don't know. I might.'

'Poor Priscilla.'

'It's poor Hamish. I don't believe you're unambitious. I think you're as big a coward as Paul Thomas. I think you're frightened of the big outside world.'

'I don't like it, I'll admit,' he said, still in that placid, happy voice which was beginning to get on Priscilla's nerves. 'If you choose to think I'm frightened, then you are entitled to your opinion. Well, there we are. Home.'

The blue lamp over the porch of the police station shone down through the rambling roses. Towser was standing on his back legs, his paws on the gate. Priscilla's car was parked outside.

'Coming in for a nightcap?' offered Hamish.

Priscilla hesitated. 'Oh, all right,' she said.

She sat in the living room while Hamish made coffee and fished out a small bottle of brandy. He stood looking at the bottle. He remembered he had bought it in the hope of just such an occasion as this. He put it on a tray along with the cups and coffee jug and two glasses and carried it through to the sitting room.

'Let's look at television,' said Hamish. 'I just want to catch what's on the news.' He switched on the set and then settled himself in the armchair after seeing that Priscilla had her coffee and brandy.

As Hamish leaned back and watched the news, Priscilla studied him. He was not only free from the pangs of ambition, but, she realized with a little shock, he was free from her. She had never known Hamish had been in love with her, but now that it was gone, she realized for the first time what was missing. Had he fallen out of love with her because of John? Was that kiss which had seemed to her exciting a big disappointment to him?

Hamish's eyelids began to droop. She leaned forward and took the brandy glass from his hand and put it on the table. In minutes, he was fast asleep. She felt she ought to leave but suddenly could not find the will to get up and go. Towser lay at her feet, snoring. The news finished and a showing of *Casablanca* came on. Priscilla sat and watched it through to the end, and then, without disturbing Hamish, she let herself out of the police station and made her way home.

Two weeks later, Hamish decided to pluck up courage and call on the Brodies. He had not seen the doctor in the pub, and heard from the gossips that the doctor had actually given up smoking.

The clammy weather had gone and the days

were crisp and sunny and cool with a hint of frost to herald the early Highland autumn.

He walked around to the Brodies' kitchen door and rang the bell.

'Walk in!' came the doctor's voice.

Angela and her husband were seated at either side of the kitchen table. He was reading a book and had a pile of books on his side of the table and his wife had her pile of books on the other and was studying one which was propped up against the jam jar. Between them lay the cat, resting its chin on top of the cheese dish.

'Oh, it's yourself, Hamish,' said the doctor. 'Help yourself to coffee and find a chair.' Angela looked up and smiled at him vaguely and returned to her books.

Hamish poured himself a cup of coffee and sat down. 'This looks like a university library,' he said.

'It is in a way,' said the doctor. 'Angela is studying for a degree in science at the Open University, and I'm getting back to my studies. I'm away behind the times.'

'You were that,' said Hamish. 'I hear you've given up smoking. Maybe Mrs Thomas did you some good after all.'

'I hate to say a good word about that woman,' said Dr Brodie. 'But I'll tell you this much, Angela recovered pretty quickly and she said she would make me one of my old breakfasts, you know, fried everything with ketchup. Well, I wolfed it down and as I was walking to the surgery, I felt downright bad-tempered and queasy. Seem to have got a taste for muesli and salads.' Hamish glanced at the title of the book the doctor had been reading, *Women and the Menopause*.

'So, I decided it was high time I moved with the times,' said Dr Brodie. 'There's a lot in this mind over matter business. I mean, I've got some patients who think they're on special tranquillizers when they're actually taking milk of magnesia tablets and yet they swear they've never felt better.'

Angela rose from the table. She was wearing quite a pretty dress and her perm was growing out. She scooped up an armful of books. 'Excuse me,' she said. 'There's a programme I want to watch on television.'

'So everything's all right,' said Hamish.

'Oh, yes, I was afraid Angela's mind was going to snap. And all over what? Some silly English housewife.'

Hamish reflected that the silly English housewife had at least stopped the doctor smoking and got him back to his medical books.

After he left them, he strolled along the waterfront. The sky was a pale green and the first star was just appearing. The peace of the world surrounded Hamish Macbeth.

Along at the harbour, the fishing boats were getting ready to set out. As he came nearer, he saw Mrs Maclean and Archie. Mrs Maclean handed her husband a packet of sandwiches and a thermos and then she put her arms about him and gave him a hug.

'Well, I neffer!' said Hamish Macbeth. He shoved his hands in his pockets and began to whistle as soft night fell and the little fishing boats with their bobbing lights made their way out to sea.

Priscilla Halburton-Smythe opened the door to her flat in Lower Sloane Street in London's Chelsea. She was feeling tired and cross. John Burlington had not turned up at the airport to meet the Inverness plane and so she had taken the underground train and it had broken down outside Acton for an hour.

She picked up the post from the doormat and carried it through to the kitchen along with a copy of the *Evening Standard* that she had bought in Sloane Square.

She flicked through the post and noticed someone had sent her a newspaper from America. She slit open the brown paper wrapper. Her friend, Peta Bently, now living in Connecticut, had sent her a copy of the *Greenwich Times*. 'See page five,' Peta had scrawled on the front of it.

Priscilla turned to page five. There was a picture of Hamish Macbeth standing with Towser under the roses outside the Lochdubh police station.

The caption read, 'Local businessman, Carl Steinberger, took this photograph of a Highland bobby while on holiday in Scotland. A far cry from *Hill Street Blues*!'

The photograph had been printed in colour.

'He might have told them about the murder,' muttered Priscilla. She unfolded the *Evening Standard*. John Burlington's face seemed to leap up at her from the front page. His face bore a tortured look and he was surrounded by detectives.

'Arrested for insider trading at his Belgravia home, stockbroker socialite, John Burlington,' Priscilla read.

The phone rang and she went to answer it.

The voice of her friend, Sarah James, came shrilly down the line. Wasn't it just too awful about poor John? As the voice went on and on, Priscilla looked out of the window. The traffic in Lower Sloane Street was belching fumes out in the air. She turned slowly and looked at the newspapers, lying side by side on the kitchen table, at the frantic face of John Burlington and at the happy face of PC Macbeth.

If you enjoyed *Death of a Perfect Wife*, read on
for the first chapter of the next book in the
Hamish Macbeth series . . .

DEATH

OF A HUSSY

Chapter One

In the Highlands in the country places
Where the old plain men have rosy faces,
And the young fair maidens
Quiet eyes.

— R.L. Stevenson

'You might have *known* people really do dress up for dinner in the Highlands.' Maggie Baird shifted her large bulk irritably in the driving seat and crashed the gears horribly.

Beside her in the passenger seat of the battered Renault 5, her niece, Alison Kerr, sat in miserable silence. Her Aunt Maggie had already gone on and on and *on* about Alison's shabby appearance before they left the house. Alison had tried to protest that, had she been warned about this dinner invitation to Tommel Castle, she would have washed and set her hair and possibly bought a new dress. As it was, her black hair was lank and greasy and she wore a plain navy skirt and a white blouse.

As Maggie Baird mangled the car on its way to Tommel Castle – that is, she seemed to wrench the gears a lot and stamp down on the footbrake for no apparent reason at all – Alison sat and brooded on her bad luck.

Life had seemed to take on new hope and meaning when her mother's sister, Maggie Baird, had descended on the hospital where Alison was recovering from lung cancer in Bristol. Alison's parents were both dead. She had, when they were alive, heard little about this Mrs Maggie Baird, except, 'We don't talk about her, dear, and want to have nothing to do with her.'

When she had thought she was about to die, Alison had written to Maggie. After all, Maggie appeared to be her only surviving relative and there should be at least one person to arrange the funeral. Maggie had swept into the patient's lounge, exuding a strong air of maternal warmth. Alison would come with her to her new home in the Highlands and convalesce.

And so Alison had been borne off to Maggie's large sprawling bungalow home on the hills overlooking the sea outside the village of Lochdubh in Sutherland in the very north of Scotland.

The first week had been pleasant. The bungalow was overcarpeted, overwarm, and over-furnished. But there was an efficient housekeeper – what in the old days would have been called a maid of all work – who came up from the village every day to clean and cook. This treasure was called Mrs Todd and although Alison was thirty-one, Mrs Todd treated her like a little girl and made her special cakes for afternoon tea.

By the second week Alison longed to escape from the house. Maggie herself went down to the village to do the shopping but she would never take Alison. Eventually all that maternal warmth faded, to be replaced by a carping bitchiness. Alison, still feeling weak and dazed and gutless after her recent escape from death, could not stand up to her aunt and endured the increasing insults in a morose silence.

Then had come the invitation to dinner from the Halburton-Smythes, local landowners, who lived out on the far side of the village at Tommel Castle, and Maggie had not told her about their going until the very last minute, hence the lank hair and the blouse and skirt.

Maggie crashed the gears again as they went up a steep hill. Alison winced. What a way to treat a car! If she herself could only drive! Oh, to be able to go racing up and over the mountains and to be free and not immured in the centrally heated prison that was Maggie's bungalow. Of course, Alison should just leave and get a job somewhere, but the doctors had told her to take it easy for at least six months and somehow she felt too drained of energy to even try to escape from Maggie. She was terrified of a recurrence of cancer. It was all very well for other people to point out that these days cancer need not be a terminal illness. Alison had had a small part of her lung removed. She was terribly aware of it, imagining a great hole lurking inside her chest. She longed daily for a cigarette and often refused to believe that a diet of forty cigarettes a day had contributed to her illness.

Maggie swung the little red car between two imposing gate posts and up a well-kept drive.

Alison braced herself. What would these people be like?

Priscilla Halburton-Smythe pushed the food around her plate and wished the evening would end. She did not like Maggie Baird, who, resplendent in a huge green and gold caftan, was eating with relish. Her voice was 'county' as she talked to Colonel Halburton-Smythe about the iniquities of poachers, and only Alison knew that Maggie had a talent for sounding knowledgeable on all sorts of subjects she knew little about.

I can't quite make her out, thought Priscilla. She's a great fat woman and quite nasty to that little niece of hers and yet Daddy is going on like an Edwardian gallant. He seems quite taken with her.

She looked again at Alison. Alison Kerr was a thin girl – well, possibly in her thirties, but such a waif that it was hard to think of her as a woman. She had thick horn-rimmed glasses, and her black hair fell in two wings shielding most of her face. She had very good skin, very pale, almost translucent. Priscilla flashed a smile at Alison who scowled and looked at her plate.

Priscilla was everything Alison despised. She was beautiful in a cool poised way with shining pale gold hair worn in a simple style. Her scarlet silk dress with the ruffled Spanish sleeves must have cost a fortune. Her voice was charming and amused.

I would be charming and amused if I lived in a castle and had doting parents, thought Alison bitterly. I know what that smile meant. She's sorry for me. Damn her.

'You will find you have to do a lot of driving in the Highlands, Mrs Baird,' the colonel said.

Maggie sighed and then looked at him with a wicked twinkle in her eyes. 'How true,' she said, 'I'm up and down that road to the village like a tart's drawers.'

There was a little silence. Mrs Halburton-Smythe opened her mouth a little and then shut it again. Then the colonel gave an indulgent laugh. 'It's not London,' he said. 'There isn't an Asian grocer at the corner of every field. You have to make lists, you know. It's quite possible to buy all the groceries for a week in one go. Doesn't that housekeeper of yours do the shopping?'

'I prefer to do it myself,' said Maggie, once more falling into the role of country gentlewoman. 'I like to get the best of everything although Lochdubh is pretty limited. I think the inhabitants must live on a diet of fish fingers.'

'You should take a trip into Inverness and stock up,' said Mrs Halburton-Smythe. 'They've got everything there now. Quite a boom town and expanding every day. Why, I remember not so long ago when it was a sleepy place and they drove the Highland cattle to market through the main street. Now it's all cars, cars, cars.'

'And crime on the increase,' said the colonel. 'What those fools in Strathbane think they're about to leave us without a policeman, I don't know.'

'Hamish!' said Priscilla. 'You didn't tell me.' She smiled at Alison. 'I only arrived last night and haven't caught up with the local news. Hamish gone? Where?'

'They've closed down the police station and taken that lazy lout off to Strathbane,' said her father. 'It's funny, I never thought Macbeth actually did anything. Now he's gone and someone has been netting salmon in the river. At least Macbeth would have found a way to stop it, although he never arrested anyone.'

'But this is dreadful,' exclaimed Priscilla. 'Hamish is a terrible loss to the village.'

'Well, *you* would naturally think so,' said her father acidly.

Priscilla's cool manner seemed ruffled. Oho! thought Alison, I wonder if the daughter of the castle is in love with the absent local copper.

Maggie looked amused. 'If you want to get him back,' she said, 'all you need to do is manufacture some crime in the village.'

She flashed a flirtatious look at the colonel. Priscilla thought, It's as if there's a beauty encased under that layer of fat.

But she said aloud, 'What a good idea. Why don't we organize a meeting in the village hall and put it to the locals.'

The colonel seemed about to protest but the suggestion caught Maggie's imagination. She liked to imagine herself a leader of Highland village society.

'I'll arrange it for you if you like,' she said. 'Alison can help. Or try to help. She's not really good at anything, you know. When shall we have the meeting?'

'Why not this Saturday?' asked Priscilla.

'You are not suggesting you are going to encourage the villagers to commit crimes so as to get Hamish back!' said Mrs Halburton-Smythe.

'Something must be done,' said Priscilla. 'We'll put it to the locals and then take a vote.'

'A vote on what?' demanded her father.

'On whatever suggestions are put up,' said Priscilla evasively. 'There's no need for you to get involved, Daddy. I am sure Mrs Baird and I can handle everything.'

Alison found herself beginning to speculate on this local bobby. He must be someone very special to attract the cool Priscilla. Her mind wandered off into fantasy. What if she helped to get him back, managed to do more than Priscilla? This Hamish Macbeth would be tall and fair and handsome like those paintings of Bonnie Prince Charlie on the old biscuit tins. He would fall in love with her, Alison, and take her away from Maggie and leave Priscilla with the knowledge that Alison's inner attractions were more important to a man than stereotyped outward beauty. She lacks character in her face, thought Alison, looking under her lashes at Priscilla and trying to find fault.

At last the evening was over. Maggie was wrapped by the butler in a voluminous mink coat. I hope Macbeth isn't into Animal Liberation, thought Alison maliciously. That coat must have taken a whole ranch of minks.

As she was leaving, the colonel suddenly leaned forward and kissed Maggie on the cheek. She flashed him a roguish look and he puffed out his chest and strutted like a bantam.

Oh, dear, thought Priscilla, I wish he wouldn't make such a fool of himself.

She did not know that her father's mis-placed gallantry was to start a chain of events which would lead to murder.

Maggie was in a good mood as she drove home through the wintry landscape and under the bright and burning stars of Sutherland. So she could still attract a man. And if she could attract a man when she was like this – well, plump – think what effect she could have if she took herself in hand.

It was all the fault of that damned waiter, thought Maggie. Maggie Baird had earned a considerable amount of money during her career. Although she had managed to stay off the streets and had been married and divorced twice, she had made a business out of being mistress to a long string of wealthy men, occa-sionally straying to the poorer ones for her own amusement. Like most women addicted to food, she also had a tremendous appetite for sex. Unlike most of her sisters on the game, she had squirrelled away her earnings, buying and selling property and investing cleverly. That was when the blow had fallen. Finding herself a very wealthy woman and looking for amusement, Maggie had taken up with a Greek waiter whose swarthy good looks had appealed to her. But for the first time in her life, she had fallen helplessly in love and when she had found that he was taking her money to save enough to marry a young blonde from Stepney, she felt her life was over.

She had bought the bungalow in the Highlands, a place to lick her wounds. She had let the bleach grow out of her hair so that it became its natural brown streaked with grey. She had put on pounds and pounds in weight. She wore tweeds and suede hats and oilskin coats and brogues and everything she could to adopt the character of a Scottish gentlewoman, as if hiding her hurt under layers of fat and country dress.

Taking Alison out of the hospital made her feel good for a while, until the novelty had worn off. Now the pain of the waiter's rejection was fading as well.

'There's life in the old girl yet,' she said cheerfully.

'You mean the car?' asked Alison.

'Me, you fool, not this heap of junk.'

'It's a very nice little car,' said Alison timidly. 'Auntie –'

'I told you not to call me that,' snapped Maggie.

'Sorry ... Maggie. Look, do you think I could take driving lessons? I could do the shopping for you.'

'I've got more to do with my money than pay for your driving lessons,' said Maggie. 'That colonel's quite a lad. His wife looks a bit of a faded nonentity. And that daughter of his! No character.'

'Exactly,' agreed Alison eagerly. Both women fell to trashing Priscilla and arrived home quite pleased with each other for the first time in weeks.

The Highlands of Scotland contain many pretty towns and villages but Strathbane was not one of them. It had been attractive once, but had become a centre for light industry in the early fifties and that had brought people flooding in from the cities. Ugly housing complexes had been thrown up all round; garish supermarkets, discos, and wine bars and all the doubtful benefits of a booming economy had come to Strathbane along with crime and drugs.

Police Constable Hamish Macbeth sadly left the kennels where his dog, Towser, was housed. It was his evening off. He was bored and lonely and he hated Strathbane and he hated Detective Chief Inspector Blair with a passion for moving him out of Lochdubh.

He was sick and tired of the youth of Strathbane with their white pinched faces, their drunkenness, and their obscenities. He was tired of raiding discos for drugs, and bars for drunks, and football matches for hooligans.

He walked along the dirty streets. A thin drizzle was falling. Even the seagulls wheeling under the harsh orange light of the sodium street lamps looked dirty. He leaned on the wall and stared down on the beach. The tide was up; oil glittered on the water and an old sofa with burst springs was slowly being gathered in by the rising tide.

A man reeled past him, then leaned against the sea wall and vomited on to the beach. Hamish shuddered and moved away. He wondered how much longer he could endure this existence. His home in Lochdubh had been the police station, so he did not even have a house to go back to. The neighbours were looking after his hens and his sheep, but he could not expect them to do so indefinitely. Some real estate agent would probably sell the police station. He had left most of his possessions there, refusing to believe his life in Lochdubh was over.

Then there was Mary Graham. PC Graham was Hamish's usual partner on the beat in Strathbane. She was a thin, spare woman with a hard face and dyed blonde hair and a thirst for making as many arrests as possible. She was from the south of Scotland and considered Hamish some sort of half-witted peasant.

Hamish's mind went back and forth and round and round the problem, seeking escape. He could always go back to Lochdubh and take lodgings with someone. He could move his hen houses on to the bit of croft land assigned to him. But, like all crofters, he knew it was impossible to live on small farming alone, trying to wrest a living out of a few stony fields. He could work on the fishing boats, of course.

What hurt most of all was that the people of Lochdubh appeared to have taken his banishment without comment. He felt very friendless.

On Saturday night, the village hall in Lochdubh was crammed to capacity. On the platform facing the audience was the committee made up of Maggie, Alison, Priscilla, and the minister, Mr Wellington, and his large, tweedy wife – who for the first time in her life was outdone in largeness and tweediness. Maggie Baird was encased in new tweeds and had a suede hat with a pheasant's feather on it on her head. Alison had washed and set her hair for the occasion, perhaps in the hope that the handsome policeman would walk in the door while the meeting was on.

Maggie Baird, much to the annoyance of Mrs Wellington, rose to speak.

'Our local policeman has been sent away because of a lack of crime in the area. I suggest we organize enough crime to make it necessary to send him back.'

There was a roar of approval. Shocked, Mrs Wellington struggled to her feet and held up her hands for silence.

'That is a most dreadful and, if you will forgive me, Mrs Baird, *immoral* suggestion.'

'What would you suggest?' asked Maggie with dangerous sweetness.

'Well, I think we should get up a petition.'

'We'll put it to a vote,' said Maggie. 'All in favour of organizing some crime, raise their hands.'

A forest of hands went up.

'All in favour of a petition?'

Only a few hands went up.

Mr Wellington took the floor. 'You cannot, Mrs Baird, expect us all to break the law.'

'No one said anything about breaking the law,' replied Maggie cheerfully. 'We make it look as if we've got a crime and insist on having the police in. I am going to pass round sheets of paper and you will all write down suggestions. I will report that something of mine, something valuable, has been stolen, and then after a bit I'll say, "Sorry to have wasted your time, it has been found." That sort of thing.'

There was a silence in the hall. Maggie realized furiously that everyone was obviously waiting for Priscilla to say something.

Feudal lot of peasants, thought Maggie angrily.

Priscilla got to her feet. She was wearing a smart grey tailored pin-striped suit with a white blouse, sheer stockings, and patent leather high heels. 'Yes, I think a bit of organized crime is the sensible answer,' said Priscilla.

'My father is having trouble again with poachers. I shall start off with that complaint.'

There was a cheer and a man shouted, 'Good for you. We knew you would think of something.'

In that moment, Alison felt quite warm toward her aunt. It did seem unfair that Maggie should have thought up the scheme only to have everyone give Priscilla all the credit.

Papers were passed around, a few half bottles of whisky were produced, the villagers scribbled busily. The air was soon heavy with the raw smell of alcohol and a fog of cigarette smoke.

When the meeting was over, everyone was happy with the results – with the exception of Mr and Mrs Wellington, Maggie, and Alison.

'Why did I bother?' fumed Maggie on the road home. 'Did you see that Halburton-Smythe bitch calmly taking the credit for everything? Anyway, my crime is the best and so I shall show them.'

Sergeant MacGregor drove angrily over the twisting Highland roads that led from Cnothan to Lochdubh. Some female had lost her diamond earrings and what should have been handled by that Macbeth fellow was now having to be handled by him, MacGregor.

What made it worse was that this female, this Mrs Baird, had phoned the high-ups in

221

Strathbane and accused them of deliberately encouraging crime in Lochdubh by taking away the village policeman and had threatened to write to *The Times*.

He drove through Lochdubh, remarking sourly to himself that it looked as sleepy as ever, and took the coast road to Maggie's bungalow.

The door was opened by a grim-looking housekeeper wearing a blue cotton dress with a white collar. MacGregor's heart sank. Anyone who could afford to employ a Scottish housekeeper these days and get her to wear a sort of uniform must be stinking rich, and stinking rich meant power, and power meant trouble.

Mrs Baird was all he had feared and anticipated. She was a great, fat woman wearing a tweed suit and heavy brogues. Her thick hair was scraped back in an old-fashioned bun and she had the glacial accents of the upper class. With her on the chintz-covered sofa sat a dab of a woman, peering at him through thick-lensed glasses, whom Mrs Baird introduced as 'my niece, Miss Kerr.'

'You took your time about getting here,' said Maggie.

'Well, I have to come from Cnothan, which is a good wee bit away,' said MacGregor with what he hoped was a placating smile.

'Stop grinning like a monkey and get your notebook out,' ordered Maggie. The housekeeper brought in a tray with a coffee pot, cream, sugar, and only two cups. MacGregor was obviously not going to be offered any.

'When did you first notice the earrings were missing?' asked MacGregor.

'Last night. I've searched the house. Mrs Todd, the housekeeper, is a local woman and above suspicion. But two suspicious-looking hikers were seen hanging about yesterday. They could have got in somehow and taken them.'

'Description?' asked MacGregor, licking his pencil.

'Man and a girl, early twenties. The man had a straggly beard and the girl looked like one of those dreary intellectual types, rather like Miss Kerr here.' Maggie laughed and Alison winced. 'The man was wearing a camouflage jacket and jeans, and the girl, a red anorak and brown slacks. The man had on a ski cap and the girl was hatless. Her hair was mousy brown.'

MacGregor eventually drove off in a more cheerful frame of mind. He had something concrete to go on. He telephoned from his Land Rover to Strathbane and put out an alert for the hikers. That strange creature, Macbeth, who had had the temerity to solve a murder case in his, MacGregor's, absence, would soon find out his presence was not missed in Lochdubh.

He had only just reached home when a call came through from the chief constable. Colonel

Halburton-Smythe demanded the presence of a policeman immediately. Poachers were netting salmon on his river. With a groan, MacGregor set out for Lochdubh again. The colonel insisted on taking the sergeant on a long walk across country to the river and haranguing him on the ineptitude of the police. MacGregor was tired and weary by the time he got back to Cnothan.

But fury gave him energy, fury generated by a call from Strathbane to say that Mrs Baird had telephoned. She had found her lost earrings down the back of the sofa and what was MacGregor doing wasting the force's time by having them look for villainous hikers who did not exist?

Then a phone call came from the Lochdubh Hotel to say that a group of young people were creating a riot in the public bar. MacGregor appealed for back-up and took the road back to Lochdubh to find the public bar empty apart from a few shattered glasses and the owner of the hotel, who was unable to give a clear description of the young people.

By the time he finally got home to bed, he was nearly in tears of rage. Morning found him in a calmer frame of mind. Lochdubh would sink back into its usual peace and quiet.

And then the phone started to ring. A crofter in Lochdubh complained that five of his sheep had been stolen during the night, and a farmer reported that two of his prize cows were missing. The schoolteacher, Miss Monson, called to say that drugs had been found in a classroom.

Again MacGregor telephoned for help, only to be asked wearily why he couldn't handle things himself – that is, until he got to the tale of the drugs in the classroom. Detective Chief Inspector Blair and a team of detectives and forensic men were despatched from Strathbane only to find that the drugs in the classroom were packets of baking soda. 'Silly me,' said the giggling schoolteacher, and Blair took his anger out on MacGregor, who had no one to take it out on except his wife, and he was afraid of her.

The amazing thing about British policewomen is that a surprising proportion of them are attractive. And so PC Hamish Macbeth could not help wondering why he had the ill luck to be saddled with such a creature as Mary Graham on his beat. PC Graham, he reflected, looked like one of those women you see in German war films. Not only was there the dyed blonde hair, but she had staring ice-blue eyes, a mouth like a trap, and an impeccable uniform with a short tailored skirt which showed strong muscular legs encased in black tights – not fine sheer tights worn by some of the younger policewomen, but thick wool ones, and her shoes were like black polished glass.

It was a sunny day as they walked side by

225

side along the waterfront, past closed bars smelling of last night's drunks; past shuttered warehouses falling into ruin, relics of the days when Strathbane was a small busy port; past blocks of houses thrown up in the fifties during that period when all architects seem to have sold their souls to Stalin, and had erected towers of concrete very like their counterparts in Moscow. The balconies had once been painted jolly primary colours, but now long trails of rust ran down the cracked concrete of the buildings in which elevators had long since died, and rubbish lay in heaps on the sour earth of what was originally intended to be a communal garden.

'I always keep ma eyes and ears open,' Mary was saying. She had a whining singsong voice. 'I hae noticed, Macbeth, you're apt to turn a blind eye tae too many things.'

'Such as?' asked Hamish while in his mind he picked her up and threw her over the sea wall and then watched her sink slowly beneath the oily surface of the rising tide.

'Two days ago there were these two drunks fighting outside The Glen bar. All you did was separate them and send them off home. I wanted to arrest them and would hae done had I not seen that wee boy acting suspiciously over at the supermarket.'

Hamish sighed. There was no point replying. Mary saw villains everywhere. But her next words nearly roused him to a fury, and it took a great deal to rouse Hamish Macbeth. 'I felt it was ma duty to put in a report about you,' she said. 'It is cramping my style to have to walk the beat wi' a Highland layabout. The trouble wi' you Highlanders is you just want to lie on your backs all day long. You know whit they say, *mañana* is too *urgent* a word for you.' Mary laughed merrily at her own wit. 'So I said I would never rise in the force, having to patrol wi' a deadbeat like you, and asked for a change.'

'That would be nice,' said Hamish.

Mary threw him a startled look. 'I'm surprised you're taking it so well.'

'Of course I am taking it well. Ye dinnae think I enjoy walking along on a fine day wi' a sour-faced bitch like you,' said Hamish in a light pleasant voice, although Priscilla, for example, would have recognized, by the sudden sibilancy of it, that Hamish was furious. 'Wass I not saying chust the other day,' said Hamish dreamily, 'that it was sore luck getting landed wi' you instead of someone like Pat Macleod.' Pat Macleod was a curvaceous brunette of a policewoman who wore sheer stockings instead of tights. Every policeman who had seen her flashing her thighs in the canteen as she deliberately hitched up her short skirt to sit down could bear witness to that.

Mary could hardly believe her ears. She would never for a moment have dreamt that PC Macbeth would even think of insulting her.

She did not know that her contempt for him was largely based on jealousy. Macbeth, in a short time, had made himself popular on the beat and householders preferred to bring their troubles to him rather than to Mary.

'I have never been so insulted in all my life,' she said.

'Oh, come now, wi' a face and manner like yours, you must have been,' said Hamish who, like all normally polite and kind people, was relishing the rarity of being truly and thoroughly rude.

'You're jist mad because Blair winkled ye oot o' your cosy number in Lochdubh,' sneered Mary. 'And you claim to have solved them murders! You! You're no' a man. I could beat the living daylights oot o' you any day.'

'Try it,' said Hamish.

She squared up to him. 'I warn ye. I'm a black belt in karate.'

'Behave yourself, woman,' said Hamish, suddenly sick to death of her.

With amazing speed, he moved in under her guard, swept her up in his lanky arms, dumped her head first in an enormous plastic rubbish bin, and, deaf to her cries, strolled off.

That's that, he thought with gloomy satisfaction, I may as well go back to the police station and resign.

The desk sergeant looked up as Hamish ambled in. 'Upstairs, Macbeth. The super's screaming for you.'

'So soon?' said Hamish, surprised. 'Did PC Graham fly in on her broomstick? Never mind. Better get it over with.'

'Come in, come in, Hamish,' said Superintendent Peter Daviot. 'Sit down, man. Tea?'

'Yes, thank you,' said Hamish, sitting down on a chair facing the desk and putting his peaked cap on his knees.

'It seems, Hamish, that there's been a bit of a crime wave in Lochdubh and Sergeant MacGregor's being run ragged.'

'Is he now?' asked Hamish with a smile. He did not like MacGregor.

'Milk and sugar? Right. Here you are. Yes, on due consideration, we have decided you should finish up the week here and return to Lochdubh. Here are the keys to the station.'

'Thank you.' Hamish felt suddenly bleak. Why had he risen to that stupid Graham woman's insults?

The door opened and Detective Chief Inspector Blair heaved his large bulk into the room. 'Oh, you're here, are you?' he said nastily when he saw Hamish.

'Yes,' said Mr Daviot. 'It seems you made a bad mistake in suggesting that Hamish be taken away from Lochdubh. There's been nothing but crime for the past few days.'

'I know,' said Blair heavily. 'I've been there on a drugs report. Baking soda, it turned oot tae be.' His Glasgow accent grew stronger in his irritation. 'Dae ye know what I think? I think them damp villagers are making up crimes so as tae get this pillock back.'

The superintendent's face froze. 'Mind your language in front of me, Mr Blair,' he said. 'Are you questioning the word of Colonel Halburton-Smythe, for example?'

'No, no,' said Blair hurriedly. 'But it did look a bit suspicious, ye ken, considering nothing happens there from the one year's end tae the other.'

'Except murder,' put in Hamish.

'Do not forget Hamish solved that woman's murder,' said the superintendent. 'I am just telling him he must go back and take up his duties there.'

'Uh-uh!' said Blair, his face creased into an unlovely smile. 'Why I came up, Mr Daviot, is to tell you we might be discussing Macbeth's dismissal from the force.'

'What! Why?'

'He assaulted PC Graham.'

'You assaulted a policewoman, Hamish?'

'It was self-defence, sir.'

'Haw! Haw! Haw!' roared Blair.

'Will you stop cackling, Blair, and give me an outline of the complaint?'

'PC Graham has just come into the station. She said she was patrolling the beat when Macbeth here suddenly picked her up and threw her in a rubbish bin.'

'Is this true, Macbeth?' No more 'Hamish.'

'She said she could beat me up and

230

approached me in a threatening manner,' said Hamish. 'I was fed up wi' her. I chust picked up the lassie and dumped her in wi' the rubbish.'

'I can hardly . . . this is very serious . . . very serious indeed. Oh, what is it, Sergeant?'

The desk sergeant had just entered. 'It's three women and a man frae the tower blocks,' he said. 'They say they've come to defend Macbeth here. They say they saw Graham attacking him and Macbeth being forced to defend himself. They say when they helped Graham out of the bin, she said she was going to get Macbeth charged with assault and they say if that's the case they will all go to court as witnesses for Macbeth's defence.'

'We must not let this get into the news-papers,' said the superintendent, horrified. 'Get rid of these people, Sergeant, and say that Macbeth is not being charged. Shut Graham up at all costs. Good heavens, just think what the tabloids could make of this. Macbeth, I suggest you go back to your quarters and pack and leave for Lochdubh in the morning. Blair, I am surprised at you! In a situation as poten-tially explosive and damaging to the police as this you should get your facts right. Macbeth, wipe that smile off your face and get going!'